THE DRACULA MURDERS

THE DRACULA MURDERS

Philip Daniels

CHIVERS
THORNDIKE

This Large Print book is published by BBC Audiobooks Ltd, Bath, England and by Thorndike Press®, Waterville, Maine, USA.

Published in 2005 in the U.K. by arrangement with the author

Published in 2005 in the U.S. by arrangement with Peter Chambers

U.K. Hardcover ISBN 1–4056–3260–7 (Chivers Large Print)
U.K. Softcover ISBN 1–4056–3261–5 (Camden Large Print)
U.S. Softcover ISBN 0–7862–7443–3 (Nightingale)

The text of this Large Print edition is unabridged.
Other aspects of the book may vary from the original edition.

Set in 16 pt. New Times Roman.

Printed in Great Britain on acid-free paper.

British Library Cataloguing in Publication Data available

Library of Congress Cataloging-in-Publication Data

Daniels, Philip.
    The Dracula murders / by Philip Daniels.
        p.   cm.
    ISBN 0–7862–7443–3 (lg. print : sc : alk. paper)
    1. Balls (Parties)—Fiction. 2. Country clubs—Fiction.
    3. Vampires—Fiction. 4. Large type books. I. Title.
    PR6054.A522D73 2005
    823'.914—dc22   2004029247

CHAPTER ONE

Count Dracula turned, his deep impenetrable eyes sweeping over the assembly with quiet malevolence. Then he pushed his way through the throng, jostling two werewolves who stood close by.

'Watch it' said one.

'Steady on, Draccy.'

He ignored them, leaning over the bar.

'Large scotch' he ordered.

Hearing the voice, a Monster turned round.

'That you, under that lot, Tommy? I'll get this. Same for me please, bartender. You look a bit needled.'

Dracula reached out for his drink.

'It's Julia again. There's some chap over there, stranger to me, dressed up in a morning suit. No make up. Says he's Van Helsing, and he can always get the better of any vampire. All balls, but Julia's encouraging him.'

'Van Helsing?' queried the Monster. 'Thought this was supposed to be a horror party. Who's he?'

The Count shrugged.

'Search me.'

Further along the bar stood two men in plain black suits, with high wing starched collars and white woollen stocks at their throats. One of them set a beer-glass down on

1

the counter.

'I must say Frank, this Burgomaster idea was a winner. Some of these chaps may look more impressive than we do, but they're sweating like hunters already, and it's only nine o'clock.'

The other man consulted his watch.

'So it is. No sign of this cabaret chap yet, is there?'

'Shouldn't worry, he's not due on till eleven. He's probably in some local graveyard, digging up corpses.'

Frank snorted.

'Listen, we don't want any second-hand corpses. This chap charges two hundred pounds for a one-hour show. For that, I expect the murders to be done live on stage, blood-draining and all.'

'I'll wander out, and see whether the boys on the door have any news of him.'

'All right Paul. I'll be in the billiard room.'

Paul Carter wended his way through the packed rooms and skirted the busy dance floor, heading for the entrance. He was feeling pleased with life at that moment. As secretary of the entertainments committee, it had been his suggestion that Halloween be celebrated, not with the usual carnival dance, with the same old boring lanterns, but with a Festival of Horror Ball. It would be expensive, both to mount and to attend. The promotion would be all-important. The impression would have to

2

be created that if you really were anyone of any status in Great Bravington, and the surrounding districts, then you would certainly appear at the ball. Twelve fifty a head might sound a lot of money, but after all, it was the Country Club's big annual do, and there was to be a reasonable buffet with a free glass of wine. On top of which, there would be a one hour presentation, by no less a performer than LeFanu the Magnificent, and everybody must realise people of that stature charge a lot of money.

There had been a lot of wrangling and infighting on the committee, not least because Carter was new to the area, and these new people mustn't think they could come barging in, and bossing everyone around. But, once the decision was made, and the Ball launched, the response had been overwhelming. Four hundred people were eager to deck themselves out as werewolves, monsters, hangmen and all manner and varieties of human oddments.

Being compelled to pass a civil word or two every few yards, Carter's progress was slow, but he finally emerged into the comparative sanity of the entrance hall. Those women had certainly gone to town on the cobwebs he thought. The overhead lighting had been switched off, and the incomer had to make do with what illumination he could get from two vast, guttering candles.

'How's it going, George?'

A short tubby man, with a gruesome eye patch and a bald-head wig, looked round.

'Oh, hello Mr. Carter. Still about forty odd ticket holders to come. Be some of the young people, I expect, having a bit of a joyride round before they descend on us.'

'I expect so. No trouble, then?'

George shook his head.

'Could have been, about half an hour ago. Gang of lads turned up on their motor bikes. Wanted to see what all the song-and-dance was about. But they had a look in, and said it was a right bore. Said it was about as exciting as a trip to the British Museum. I'm only repeating what they said.'

Carter laughed.

'That's all right, George. I'm glad they took that attitude. We both remember the upset at the tennis do, don't we?'

'Gawd, yes. Don't want another night like that.'

There was a scream of delighted terror behind them, and a young dark-haired girl burst into the hall from the restaurant. Behind her appeared a threatening Dracula, his lips pulled back to reveal the long fangs at either side of his mouth. The girl's tight little breasts heaved up and down, as she panted for breath. One final shriek, and she fled out into the night. Dracula winked briefly at George as he rushed after her.

'Should have brought our fangs, George,'

4

observed Carter solemnly.

'Don't think they'd do me much good, at my age. That's four Draculas out there already. Plus two Frankensteins and a Werewolf. They've started early tonight. Must be this Transylvanian wine.'

'That'll be it,' Carter agreed. He had personally supervised the removal of the supermarket labels, and the pasting on of the crude, authentic-looking stickers of the black castle. 'You must make a fortune in second-hand underwear after these dos.'

'You'd be surprised. Do you know, two years ago, I actually found a pair of trousers on the third tee. Trousers. How did the bloke ever explain that? We hung up a notice in the members bar, you know. They never were claimed. Caused a few jokes round here, I can tell you.'

Carter's smile was less warm. He didn't like to be reminded of celebrated events that occurred before his time.

'This chap, Le Fanu the Magnificent, ought to be here any minute now. Head him off, will you George? Don't want him going through the club, it'll spoil his impact. Try to get him to go round the back, through the changing rooms.'

George nodded importantly.

'Don't you worry, Mr. Carter. I'll take him round myself.'

'Well, I'll see you later.'

'Right.'

Carter went away. George picked up a half-empty beer-glass from behind a witches hat. I'll see you later, he said. Like hell he would. This might be the biggest night of the year, but some things never changed. Unless there was a fight, or a row of some kind at the entrance, George would see no more of Carter, or any committee man, until it was going home time. He'd sit out here, hour after hour, by himself. Later on, a drunk would come and join him. Somebody who wanted to get away from the booze and the heat. Somebody who would talk utter rubbish for a quarter of an hour, then disappear back inside. George had spent many a long night like this one, and knew exactly what to expect.

Or so he had thought.

The outer door opened and a man stepped inside. A little above medium height, about five feet ten, his frame was thin to the point of emaciation, and the undertaker's suit hung about him in folds. Long bony hands protruded like claws from the sleeves of his coat. But it was the face that startled the doorkeeper. Long and pointed, with deep-set burning eyes recessed behind flaps of parchment skin. Thin cadaverous cheeks, with a small sharp nose, and a tiny black slit of a mouth. His skin had the unnatural whiteness of death.

If they were giving a costume prize in there,

thought George, there'd be no arguments about the winner.

'Mr. Le Fanu?' he asked.

The eyes seemed to bore into him, making him uncomfortable.

The man spoke, in a dry, hissing voice.

'Is that some kind of humorous observation?'

'Er no, I was expecting—that is—'

'My ticket.'

He took the printed ticket reluctantly from the spidery fingers.

'Not Mr. Le Fanu then?'

'No.'

'Then who—'

George stopped speaking at the sight of those awful eyes.

'Is the ticket in order?'

'Oh yes, quite.'

'Is it part of your duties to announce the guests?'

'No. No, it isn't.'

'Then who I am is none of your concern.'

The newcomer stalked past him and into the club. George shivered. Colder out here than he'd thought. What a creepy character. He'd certainly entered into the spirit of the thing. Bit too much to suit some of us.

Inside, people who caught sight of the latest arrival nudged each other, muttering. Somehow, a path was made for him. Where sweating waiters had to plead and push, there was suddenly space enough for this man to go through, without touching anyone. Women who saw him shrank back instinctively, if he came too close. The men attempted half-hearted sniggers, but these were mostly stillborn. He left a trail of chilled silence in the bar as he went into the ballroom.

'Damned good,' exclaimed a balding Executioner, after he'd gone.

'Good?'

'That chap. Really very good indeed. It is a Horror Ball, isn't it? They promised us a bit of a scare, in all the publicity. I thought it was just advertising, but that fellow definitely gave me a bit of a turn. Don't mind admitting it.'

A woman giggled nervously.

'He was rather rich, wasn't he? Those eyes. I swear if he'd looked down the front of my dress, they'd have shrivelled up.'

'No fear of that, Maggie. Too much good material there.'

A red-haired Witch turned to her companion.

'Oh well, if we're back to Maggie's tits again, I think we can assume the party is restored to normal.'

The hubbub in the bar resumed at its previous level.

At the sides of the ballroom, the lights were subdued. The arrival of the man with the death mask face went almost unnoticed, and he stood beside a gold plush curtain, watching.

8

Sidney Page's Original Foxtrot Orchestra were blowing away, in a fair imitation of a nineteen-twenties arrangement. Three saxophones, two trumpets and one trombone, playing in the clipped close-harmony phrasing of those long-dead days, while behind them, an old-fashioned string bass and a banjo plucked out the rhythm, alongside a drummer and pianist. The latest dance craze was the Stamp, and one of the trumpet-players now stood up from his chair, and picked up an amplified megaphone, which he placed to his lips.

'You got to treat that lady
Just like she was a tramp
Everybody stamp.
C'mon and STAMP.'

And stamp they did. It was a bizarre sight. Every known horror figure was represented many times over, some of them twenty and thirty times. To watch their laughing, sweating faces, as they brought down their feet in unison to the singer's commands, created an atmosphere reminiscent of party time in Dante's Inferno.

'Ain't no good to stand there
Like something's got the cramp
Everybody stamp
C'mon and STAMP.'

9

Crash went the feet. Over went a few more glasses on tables placed too close to the dance area.

'Clumsy sod.'

A Catwoman limped off, pursued by an anxious Frankenstein.

'Just an accident, Myra.'

'Ought to be more bloody careful. I think you've broken something.'

They went past the standing man, too absorbed in their own little drama to notice him.

'Everybody stamp
C'mon now Stamp.'

If those eyes had glittered before, they were burning coals now. The man gave a long, drawn-out hiss, and began to push his way through the shrieking stamping mob. One prancing Demon swung round angrily as he was knocked off balance, but subsided as he found himself looking into that ghastly face. Others too, became suddenly subdued as the intruder paused. But they were only a handful out of the huge, frenzied throng, who continued to stamp and shout on cue.

There were three steps at the side of the stand, and up there the man advanced. The singer saw him coming, and looked anxiously at the leader, who shrugged. Probably some club official, he decided, about to announce the tombola or something. Not a bad time for it. The crowd could do with the quiet after all this excitement.

'Last chorus,' he called out.

Blast the man, he was standing in the front of the band, right in the way of the singer, who grinned half-heartedly and stepped to one side, raising the megaphone, only to find his voice dying in his throat. He felt powerless to carry on in the face of that ominous presence. The music faltered, as one musician after another felt himself drawn under the spell of the death-figure standing there.

At first, the dancers carried on. Then, those nearest to the band gradually realised the driving insistent rhythm had faltered, and was now stopped. Looking enquiringly for the reason they became aware of a black-clad figure towering above them and staring down. There was something remote, something that was cold and evil, knifing through the atmosphere of boisterous good humour. The feeling spread quickly, and soon the whole ballroom was still.

'Play up.'

'One more time, Sidney.'

'Everybody STAMP.'

'Shut up, Jack. Be serious, for a minute.'

The spectre raised his arms sideways, the bony talons of his fingers seeming to reach out in an embracing death-grasp. Several of the women gasped.

11

'I am Nosferatu.'

'Who did he say?'

'Nos—something, I think.'

'Who's that, then?'

'Listen.'

Although his voice was not loud, the low hissing tone penetrated every corner of the room, like some verbal snake slithering through the listeners' consciousness.

'I am Nosferatu,' it repeated. 'Spokesman for the Council. The Council of the Undead.'

Someone laughed, but was shushed at once by a dozen others.

'Ye mock at those who cannot rest. Those who lie uneasy in their graves. Cease now. Desist from your foolish meddling. The powers of darkness shall seek terrible retribution if ye persist. Go now, before it is too late. The Undead are among you, even now. Go to your homes, and seek the forgiveness of Beelzebub, the Prince of Night.'

'I don't like this, George.'

'No. Quite right. Chap's going too far.'

Suddenly, a broad-shouldered man jumped up on to the stand, confronting the hissing man.

'Look here, Mr. Whoever-you-are, you're going a bit too strong. Making some of these ladies nervous. Joke's a joke, and all that, but we've had enough. Come on now Sidney, play up, and let's get on with the fun.'

'Hear, hear.'

12

'That's the stuff, John.'

But the black-clad phantom ignored the interruption.

'Hear me. Hear Nosferatu. I bring you terrible warning. Listen, do you not hear the rustling? The stuttering of the feet of rats in the eaves? The hoot of the owl? The night creatures know. They feel the stalking of the Undead—'

'Right, that's enough. Come on, some of you fellows. Give me a hand with him. Freddie, up you come, and you, Mike.'

Half a dozen assorted figures jumped up on the platform, and began to hustle the speaker away. The first man, John, turned to address the crowd. Nasty do, that. This binge was finished if he didn't do something.

'Ladies and gentlemen, I'm not on the committee or anything, so I can honestly say I don't claim any of the credit. I don't know about you, but I've had a damned good fright, and I think our entertainer deserves a jolly good round of applause. He certain had me fooled for a minute, and probably a few more, I suspect. He said he was from the Council of the Undead. I think that's another name for the Lower Bravington Rural District Council. Chap's really a rate-collector, you know.'

'Ought to be a grave-digger.'

The speaker turned to the band-leader.

'Can you give us something with plenty of noise?'

'Number Sixty Two,' called out the pianist, turning over his music.

'The band's ready to play, ladies and gentlemen, but I think we ought to show our appreciation for that little bit of fun.'

John began to clap. Others joined in, half-heartedly at first. Then, as relief swept through the hall, the applause swelled and became deafening, with catcalls and whistles from all sides.

'Play up Sidney, and for God's sake make it loud.'

The band roared into life. John smiled and waved at the crowd, walking off.

'Good old John.'

'Trust John to know what to do. D'you know, that act was so good, I quite forgot he was entitled to a clap.'

John dismounted from the platform, where Paul Carter was waiting for him.

'I want to thank you John, for what you did.'

'No trouble, old boy. Creepy bastard, wasn't he? What was all that about, do you know?'

'Not a clue. I was in the bar when he started, so I only heard half of it.'

'Put the squitters up one or two people, I can tell you. Fellow ought to be locked up. Ah, here's Mike. What did you do with him, Mike? Shoved him headfirst down the nearest bog, I trust?'

Mike grinned.

'Wanted to, old boy. No, we got him to a

14

side-door, and just heaved him out. Didn't like touching him, somehow. Made me feel as if I'd like a bath.'

'Know what you mean. Something unclean about the fellow.'

Paul Carter spoke then.

'Well gentlemen, I can't do you a bath, just at the moment. But I should be very glad if you'd join me in a large glass of what cures it.'

'Good idea.'

At the entrance, George the doorkeeper was surprised to find himself joined suddenly by two of the younger committee members.

'Just had to chuck some lunatic out, George. We'll stay with you for a bit, in case he tries to get back in.'

In the ballroom, the crowd were delighted, as waiters appeared suddenly, bearing free champagne.

'I say, free bubbly. Pretty magnanimous.'

'Purely medical darling. They say if you pour a good vintage on a vampire's tail, he disappears.'

'Well, I'm going to pour mine down my throat. Never know when you might swallow a vampire's tail.'

'I didn't know vampires had tails.'

In the billiard room, Frank Beamish sat, drawing on his pipe.

'Nasty do, that, Frank,' said his companion.

'M'm. Thank God old John Matthews jumped in when he did. Saved the day.

15

Wonder who that fellow was?'

'Some nut-case. Probably escaped from somewhere, judging by the way he carried on. Think we should tell the police?'

Frank took the pipe from his mouth, and spoke firmly.

'Absolutely not. What could we say? Somebody came to a horror party, and frightened people? Would sound a bit daft, wouldn't it? Besides, it would get us publicity of the wrong kind. No, I think we'll do better to leave it alone. Let people think it was an act, or a joke, or whatever they like. Don't forget, we might want to run another one of these some time.'

The other man groaned.

'Not if I have to wear a bloody wolf's head again.'

The murderer lifted back his head, and gazed down.

Pale moonlight flickered across the ashen face beneath him, the face of a young girl, her eyes frozen in horror.

'Lucy, oh Lucy,' he breathed. 'Speak now. Come with me. Be my bride. Dwell with me forever in eternal light. The blood of a new-born babe shall be our feast. Speak now, my love.'

The terrified eyes did not move.

He felt the hotness rising in him, like a burning fever that spread through every fibre, reaching out to his fingertips. Redness invaded

16

his mind, as the roaring in his ears built up to a tremendous crescendo.

'Now Lucy, speak, I command it.'

But there was no answer, and the redness torrented out from him, in a great, spilling thrust.

He lay there, drained.

Anger now. Anger, cold and deadly, seeping through every vein with tendrils of ice.

'You defy me. You defy Dracula, Prince of Darkness. It is a sign. A sign that you are not chosen. You seek to betray me. Die.'

Rearing back, he towered above her for a fraction of time. Then his clenched hands came down with maniacal force. An owl hooted in the distance.

The timely intervention by John Matthews, combined with the immediate distribution of free champagne, had quite restored the ball to its previous gaiety. Le Fanu the Magnificent had arrived in good time, and been persuaded to put on his show thirty minutes early. It was good old-fashioned, magic, with suitable touches of horror, and aided by eerie, taped music and stroboscopic lighting.

'How did he make that girl's head float across the stage?' queried an ageing Demon.

'Wires, old boy. All wires.'

'H'm,' doubtfully. 'Well, I could understand that, in a London theatre. But we're a bit short of theatrical doo-dahs in this club, you know.'

'Got to be wires. I say, what about some

more of the old vampire juice?'

A worried-looking young Catwoman approached a noisy group.

'Anyone seen Liz?' she queried.

An evil-masked Mr. Hyde looked around.

'Oh hallo, Jeannie. Good party, isn't it? Liz? No. Haven't seen her. You know what they say. Cherchez la Tony.'

'Le Tony,' reprimanded his companion. 'Masculine, old man. Anyway, that won't do. I saw Tony outside just now, soaking his head.'

'That'll make his fangs drop out.'

Jeannie clucked with impatience.

'Listen, I wish you'd be a bit serious. Liz is not here. I haven't seen her for nearly an hour.'

Mr. Hyde looked at her, with a very sober expression.

'Jeannie, old love, I have been meaning to have a talk with you, for some time past. You're growing up, Jeannie, and it's time we spoke about men. They can be very evil people, men, where pretty girls are concerned. You say Liz is missing? Look around. So are a dozen others. Where are they, you ask? Where, indeed, but with men? Men who pursue, for their own base desires. With fast motor cars, wine and etchings. And the tool of the trade of lecher.'

A nearby Dracula interrupted.

'That ought to be tools, surely?'

'Silence, old vampire. I'm giving this

18

lecture.'

'Oh, it's no use talking to you lot. You're all half-pissed. Somebody go and get Tony out of the loo. He'll take a proper interest.'

'Right you are.'

A Wizard went off in search of Tony. Count Dracula leered at the worried girl.

'I say Jeannie, while they're getting him, don't fancy a spot of neck-chewing, do you?'

Jeannie smiled, despite her concern.

'Ask me again when you're sober. We'll see.'

'Lovely.'

The Wizard was back, looking worried.

'I say Jack, spare me a minute, will you? Scuse us, Jeannie.'

'Yes, but what about Tony?' she called after them.

Dracula Jack whispered to the Wizard.

'This had better be important. I was just starting to chat Jeannie up. What's all the excitement, anyway?'

'You'll see.'

They went into the men's cloakroom. Slumped in a quickly-imported armchair was another Dracula, his dinner-jacket smeared with mud, and pieces of grass. There was blood on his face.

'Ye gods,' whistled Jack. 'What happened to him?'

'Can't get any sense out of him. Says he must have fallen over. Suppose he must have done. He's still half-stoned. Point is, how do

19

we get him home? Can't let them see him in there.'

'What do you mean, get him home? We can't let his family see him, either.'

The Wizard snorted.

'Well, what's the answer, then? Leave him here till the morning, or what?'

Jack thought for a moment.

'We'll get him to his car. Go out through the changing rooms.'

'He can't drive, in this condition.'

'I know that. We'll take his keys. Stretch him out on the back seat. Tell everyone he went home early. Give me a hand with him, Bas.'

Bas nodded.

'I don't like it, but it'll do for a start—Hallo, what's that?'

From the ballroom behind them came the high-pitched screaming of a woman.

CHAPTER TWO

It was two forty five a.m. when Superintendent Vine marched into the entrance hall of the Great Bravington Country Club. His eyes took in the forlorn groups of people, standing around in an odd assortment of street clothes and fancy dress. The muttering ceased as he entered, and everyone looked at him with interest.

'Who is in charge here, please?'

His voice was pleasant. Damned pleasant, he thought, for a chap who's been dragged out of bed and had to drive fifty miles in the middle of the night.

'Excuse me sir, would it be Mr. Vine?'

A medium-sized, elderly man stood in front of him.

'I'm Vine, yes,' he acknowledged.

'Very good, sir. This way, if you please. I'm George, the caretaker.'

He was led through a bar—now closed, he noted from habit—where more people sat around, making desultory conversation, or just staring at the floor. Poor sods. Nice way to end a party.

George knocked on a panelled door, and opened it.

'Mr. Vine, sir.'

Vine nodded his thanks and stepped inside.

A man clutching a pipe stood up to greet him. So did another, younger man, the only one present who wasn't dressed up for a party.

'Frank Beamish, the club president.'

'Inspector Cornwell, sir.'

Both men spoke at once, Vine looked at each in turn, and made up his mind quickly.

'Mr. Beamish, I realise this is a terrible situation for the club. Now that I'm here, I'll get done with the formalities as fast as ever I can. No need to distress your members any longer than we have to.'

21

Beamish wagged his head, worriedly.

'I'm glad you at least appreciate that, superintendent. I've been trying to convince the inspector this past hour.'

Vine looked at the inspector, who stared back impassively.

'Quite. Well now, as to the inspector, let me reassure you, Mr. Beamish. What he has done, by keeping everyone here, has been entirely correct. And, let me point out, it has saved the club and the town a good deal of embarrassment.'

The club official raised his eyebrows.

'How so?'

'Because, by causing an hour or two of inconvenience now, we can eliminate the vast majority of the guests from future enquiries. If they'd been allowed to go, it would have meant an incessant stream of police cars, roaming all over the town, for the next couple of days. Calls at people's homes, their offices. Very time-consuming, and very wasteful too, for all concerned. Think about it Mr. Beamish. In the cold light of day, you'll probably decide to make the inspector an honorary member.'

Well said, thought Cornwell. Don't often get such a strong back-up from the big brass.

'Now Mr. Beamish,' resumed the superintendent. 'You're in authority here, and you know everyone. I wonder if you would mind passing around the word? Tell them I'm here, and who I am. Say that most of them will

22

be on their way home in half an hour, after leaving their names and addresses. No doubt the club would want to make coffee available, if anyone wants it?'

'Oh, certainly.'

Glad of some action at least, Beamish smiled and strode out.

Vine closed the door behind him, and sat down close by the leather-topped desk. Eyeing his junior thoughtfully, he said.

'You took a bloody fine chance, getting me out of bed. Mind telling me why?'

Cornwell had been expecting something of the kind.

'Yes sir. This is the most important social centre in the town. These people here tonight, they run the place. They're all worried about scandal, about their good names, and the rest of it. There'll be a lot of head-wagging going on, for miles around. Tomorrow, the press'll be in here like a pack of wolves. I knew this would have to come to you eventually. Might have been too late for all kinds of reasons. I decided to contact you myself. Direct.'

'H'm.' Good chap, this Cornwell. Clear-thinking. 'Well, you must know you'll get bollocked up hill and down dale for jumping the system. Quite right, too. On the other hand, I might not have heard this till lunch-time, or worse. Now I'm here, ahead of the press and the big coppers' boots. That's good. As far as I'm concerned, you did the right

23

thing, inspector.'

'Thank you, sir.'

Vine looked at him quizzically. Mustn't have him preening himself.

'But you'll get bollocked, just the same. Right, enough of that. What's the story?'

'A young woman was murdered. Elizabeth Warren, aged nineteen. Her father is a partner in a firm of local solicitors.'

'Oh Gawd.'

'She was stabbed through the heart, sir. Odd weapon. An arrow. The kind you buy in the sports shops. Brass-tipped job. Oh, and the head had been snapped off.'

'Arrow, eh?' You're quite right, it is an odd weapon. Take a bit of strength to push it in, as well. Go on.'

'The murder was committed approximately sixty yards from the clubhouse, on clear ground, but there is a clump of bushes in between, which would obscure the view from here.'

'Time?'

'Between nine thirty and eleven, sir.'

The inspector waited for the storm.

'What do you mean, between nine thirty and eleven?' Vine said nastily. 'Crowded place, people coming and going all the time.'

'Just so, sir. Probably when we've collected statements we'll be able to narrow it down—'

'—bloody hope so—'

'—but the trouble is, with a party of this

24

kind, well, people do tend to go missing. Young people, especially.'

'So everybody decided she was having it off outside, and didn't bother about her.'

'Perhaps if I tell you the rest of our findings, sir?'

Vine grunted.

'Come on, then.'

'The dead girl came with a partner, Tony Benson, aged twenty two. They've been going around together for some months. Benson got rather drunk. Two of his friends found him in the cloakroom. His clothes were muddy, and there was blood on his face. This was before anyone knew about Miss Warren's death. They decided the best thing to do was to put him in his car, let him sleep it off.'

'Bloody idiots. He might have driven off, and killed somebody.'

'Well sir, yes and no.'

'What's that supposed to mean? Don't play riddles, inspector. It's three o'clock in the bleeding morning.'

'Sorry sir. These friends did the sensible thing. They took Benson's keys away from him. Unfortunately, for all concerned, there was a spare key in the glove compartment. He must have come round, and decided to leave. There's a T-junction about half a mile away. He went straight across it and smashed into an oak tree on the other side.'

'Bad, is he?'

'He's dead, sir.'

Vine pulled out a packet of cigarettes, and lit one. 'Christ, what a mess. Why wasn't I told about this boy?'

Cornwell shook his head.

'Not possible, sir. He was only found an hour ago. You were already on your way. The body was taken by the emergency down to the county mortuary. Some alert character down there had the bright idea of notifying the people running the ball.'

Vine blew out an irritable stream of smoke.

'Let me get this straight. These youngsters came to the dance together. The boy got drunk. We don't know exactly when. The girl went missing, and perhaps young Benson as well. The girl is murdered. Benson is discovered with his clothes in a state. When he comes to, he drives off at a hell of a lick. Fast enough to get himself killed, anyway. Is that it?'

'That's it exactly, superintendent.'

'Well, I must say it sounds good. Bit of a quarrel, chap loses his temper. Is that what you're thinking, inspector?'

Cornwell spoke with some care.

'As you say sir, it sounds good. But the arrow. A man who really loses control will certainly grab anything that's to hand. But arrows don't often come to hand.'

Vine grunted.

'Fancy dress do, though. Perhaps he was

26

Robin Hood?'

'No sir, it isn't that kind of fancy dress. All horror characters. Young Benson came as Count Dracula.'

'Another one? I must have seen three of those on the way in. Looks a bit daft with a sheepskin coat on. Still, I take your point. Rum thing to use. Just the same, I fancy the boy for this job. How many men have you got here?'

'One sergeant, two constables.'

'With the chap who drove me, that's four. Have you weeded out the people I'll have to talk to tonight?'

'Best I can, sir. Rather a lot, I'm afraid.'

Vine ground out his cigarette.

'Well, let's get on with it. Get the others on names and addresses. If any of the guests thinks he saw something, add them on to my squad.' He raised his voice, as someone knocked at the door. 'Who is it?'

A young man put his head round.

'Are you the inspector?'

He looked from one to the other. Cornwell spoke.

'I am Inspector Cornwell, but the senior officer in charge here is Superintendent Vine.'

'Oh.' He turned his gaze on Vine.

'And your name please?' queried the super.

'Woodley. I'm Charles Woodley.'

'Well, Mr. Woodley, we're really rather busy. What can we do for you?'

'I think I saw the murderer.'

Vine looked across sharply.

'We'd better get Mr. Woodley a chair, inspector.'

Cornwell hastened to place a chair in position between them. Woodley sat down, his face anxious.

'Now, Mr. Woodley, this is of the utmost importance, as I'm sure you appreciate. You say you may have seen the murderer? Suppose you tell us all about it, in your own words.'

*   *   *

Charles Woodley—or Young, as he was inevitably known—was not enjoying the Festival of Horror Ball. In fact, it would not be overstating the case to say that he wished fervently he had stayed in bed for the whole day.

It had begun with a late-morning row. His father had returned to the house after an early round of golf, to find that Charles was still in bed. After a few exchanges, he had risen, and made straight for the Feathers, the usual gathering place of the Turks before an away game. There'd been no time for lunch, of course, and he'd set off for the fixture, even before the pub shut. Convinced that he knew a route which would avoid not only the motorway, but even the A-roads, he had launched himself on an intricate pattern of side-roads, some of them little better than

28

cart-tracks. When the car broke down, it took him over an hour to find any assistance, and he finally arrived at the opposition ground when the game was past the halfway mark, and the Turks eight points behind.

This put him into a frame of mind where he could do nothing right. Fumbled passes and mis-kicks became the order of the day, and the humiliation of his team was complete.

'Stop worrying, Young.'

'Just one of those days, old boy.'

But he had not been comforted, and was in two minds about whether to give the horror party a miss. However, at twelve pounds fifty a ticket, he really couldn't afford the gesture, and in any case Sue would have played hell. In the event, he donned his Satan costume, collected Susan Ainsworth, and reported for the shindig.

To his relief, it was rather better organised than he had expected, and there was an unpredicted bonus. In the fancy dress he was Satan, and not Young Woodley who completely let down the Turks that afternoon. In a dinner jacket, he would have felt that people were pointing him out, and nudging each other.

This Transylvanian wine was a bit of a find, too. Not your usual supermarket plonk, by any means.

Susan said to him crisply,

'Charles, I want you to do two things for

29

me.'

'Absolutely, old girl. I say, what a smashing dress. Won't fall off, will it?'

'That's the fourth time you've asked me. It's becoming a bore. Now, these two things. Are you listening to me?'

'Full attention, ma'am. Hundred per cent.'

'Right. For Pete's sake stop maundering on about that blasted game today. I am sick to death of it.'

'Will do. At once. What about Two?'

'Two. Stop packing that stuff away. You've eaten nothing all day, and you'll regret it.'

He was offended.

'Oh come now. You're not seriously suggesting a grown man can't drink two or three glasses of this stuff?'

'You've had five glasses while I've watched you. And if I know you, an extra one or two on your way around the clubhouse.'

He had promised, with utmost seriousness. At ten o'clock, he was sitting alone at the end of the bar, explaining to the bartender that one particular pass hadn't come to him quite as cleanly as Miffy Horton was telling everybody. Susan had been gone for over half an hour, and he had scarcely noticed. It wasn't long after that, when the room began to shift and swirl around him in a most alarming way.

'Why don't you slip out for some fresh air, sir? Getting a bit stuffy in here.'

Outside, the recommended fresh air did

him no good at all. Moon and clouds, trees and bushes, all seemed to whirl and cavort in some abandoned dance. Young Woodley lurched forward twenty yards, sideways another six, and then was violently ill.

'Who is that animal?'

'Can't tell, love, not in that get-up.'

Dimly grateful for his protective costume, Woodley went further into the darkness, bumped into someone, apologised, and found himself addressing a tree. Slithering down to the base, he fell thankfully asleep.

When he awoke, the air had cleared his head somewhat. The confusion had disappeared, to make way for a dull, insistent thudding. He wished he hadn't woken at all, then became urgently aware of the reason. Scrambling to his feet, he looked around. Bit too near the club, he decided. Pushing in through a clump of bushes, he made certain he couldn't be seen from behind, then relieved himself. So intent had he been on his need, that he hadn't before seen what he now saw, not many yards away.

A couple were stretched out on the grass. He couldn't make out who they were, except that the man must be one of the many Draculas, judging by the rich heavy cape he was wearing. They seemed to be making lovetalk. Woodley couldn't distinguish any of the conversation, except that the man kept calling out the girl's name. Fascinated at first, he suddenly became aware that he was about to add the disgusting crime of Peeping Tom to whatever awful list he'd already compiled that night. Turning away, he picked his careful quiet path back towards the clubhouse.

*   *   *

Inspector Cornwell's ballpoint pen had been working overtime.

Superintendent Vine said,

'I think I may have misheard you, Mr. Woodley. You said this man kept repeating the girl's name. Did I understand you to say Lucy?'

'That's right. Lucy. Over and over again.'

Vine frowned.

'The young woman who was murdered was named Elizabeth. It couldn't have been Lizzy, could it? Or Liz?'

But Woodley was not to be shaken.

'Absolutely not,' he said firmly. 'Lucy. Not once, but many times.'

'I see. Well, we're very much obliged for your cooperation. Like you to make a statement, if you would. Just for the record, you understand. Make everything tidy. Could you come down to the station tomorrow, or I should say later today? Pick a time to suit yourself.'

'Yes. Of course. Certainly.'

'Thank you, Mr. Woodley. Meantime, keep

32

going over that scene in your mind. Concentrate on the man. Anything you can tell us, anything at all, might be important. Might not seem so to you, but we'd be very glad to know it, believe me.'

Woodley went out. Cornwell looked expectantly at his chief.

'Well, what do you make of all that, inspector?'

'Not much for us, sir. Pity he didn't go over and interrupt.'

'Ha. Would you? The best you could hope for would be a black eye. And probably the girl would be the one to give it to you, these days.'

'True enough, sir,' smiled the inspector. 'What about this name business, this Lucy? He was pretty adamant about that.'

The superintendent nodded.

'Yes, he was. But I'm not going to take too much notice. Don't forget, he was still fairly pissed, by his own admission. If the girl's name had been Betty or Joan I'd have been a lot more interested. But the difference between Lucy and Lizzy several yards away, to a mind already fuddled by booze, well, I ask you. Speaking of the girl, why aren't her parents here, demanding action?'

'They're away for a couple of days, sir. I've sent word.'

'Poor devils.' Vine looked at his watch. 'Mr. Woodley's delayed us a bit. You said on the phone that those idiots carried the body inside.

33

If there was anything to find out there, they probably ruined it with their big feet.'

'I marked it out as best I could sir, in the dark.'

'Well, not your fault. I'd better take a look at her, and then we'll get the interviews going.'

'Right sir. She's in the visitors' changing room. There's a proper first aid bed in there.'

'Doctor?'

'Our own man only arrived a few minutes before you, sir. There were a couple of G.P.s among the guests. They took charge until he came.'

'Good. Lead the way.'

CHAPTER THREE

She lay awkwardly on a hard canvas bed. Her eyes were fixed in a stare of pure horror. The dress had been pulled down, to expose her breasts, a final touch of shocked indecency to her pathetic body. A bloody wooden obscenity protruded from her.

She was Elizabeth Warren, aged nineteen.

And she was dead.

Superintendent Vine stared down at her, his face a mask. No one could begin to guess, by looking at him, that there was anything but professional detachment inside his head. They weren't to know that Superintendent Vine had twin daughters aged twenty, and that he was visualising each of them in turn, lying in place of the murdered girl. There was no sign of troubled anger in his mind, when he spoke.

'Can you report yet, doctor?'

He thought the question was rhetorical. A man didn't need seven years' medical training before he could spot the murder weapon.

The official examiner was a bristle-headed, red-faced man with years of county work behind him. His name was George Whatmore, and they'd met many times in the course of duty. To Vine's surprise, he showed some reluctance.

'Not quite, superintendent. The light in here is not really good enough. I'll have to examine her thoroughly when we can get her down to the mortuary.'

Vine arched his eyebrows.

'Well yes, of course, quite understand that, doctor. But, cause of death, I mean, that's easy enough, surely?'

Whatmore fiddled in his pockets.

'Done all I can for the moment. Care to join me outside for a cigarette?'

About to remonstrate, Vine caught the doctor's eye.

'Yes, good idea. Seems a bit callous, smoking in here.'

Outside, they walked onto the grass.

'What's bothering you, doctor?'

'Probably nothing. I may be making a fuss.

If I am, I don't want those other chaps to know. Good doctors, and all that, but they're not coroner's men, don't know all our little ways. And I certainly don't want to rouse their suspicions.'

'Suspicions? What about?'

'About the cause of death.'

Vine stopped in mid-stride, and stared at him.

'Cause of—you'd better go on, I think.'

The doctor nodded, chewing at his lower lip.

'Yes. Well, as I say, the lighting in there is bad. But I didn't like the look of the blood around the wound. There's not enough of it to suit me, for a start.'

'Not enough? But you wouldn't expect a lot, surely? Good hard thrust like that?'

'Not a lot, I agree. But a young woman like that, in prime condition, ought to have bled rather more than she did. And then again, even in that light, the clothing doesn't seem right. Not the right texture. As I say, I shall need lab conditions.'

Vine was thoughtful. Doctor George Whatmore was a man with a lot of experience. If he said he needed more tests, it wasn't a matter of professional fussiness. The man was plainly worried.

'Doctor, there's no one around to overhear. Do me a favour, and stick your neck out. It might be a great help to me in the early stages

36

of my investigation. What do you suspect? I won't quote it against you believe me.'

'Well,' Whatmore hesitated, even then. But he had known Vine for some years, and after all, if it was going to help him . . . 'All right. It's possible, and I only say possible, that the girl was already dead, or dying, when that arrow was driven into her.'

'Wow.'

They resumed walking, in silence. The policeman's mind was busy adjusting to this new information.

'You're suggesting therefore that death was due to some other cause. But what? Are there any other visible wounds? I'm assuming we can rule out heart failure.'

The doctor shook his head.

'We can't rule out anything at all. For all I know, the young woman may have a heart history, although I should be surprised to hear it.'

'What, then?'

'It could be some form of poison,' Whatmore admitted reluctantly.

'My God. Life is going to be difficult, if you're right. But why would a chap want to attack someone who's already dead?'

'I'm sorry, superintendent. That is police work, and you know far more about that than I do. I can only give you such facts as come to light.'

'Yes, I understand. But you've shaken me a

37

bit, I must confess. Still, as you say, that's my worry. Anything else you can tell me? Subject to your lab work, of course.'

Whatmore flicked away his cigarette, in a high glowing arc.

'There'd been some love play. The girl's lips are slightly bruised, and there's a love bite on her neck. Rather a nasty one, as a matter of fact, drew blood. And there was some attempt at intercourse.'

Vine was very alert.

'Attempt?'

'Yes. It doesn't look as though entry was effective.'

'I see. Was the girl a virgin?'

The doctor strove to keep impatience from his voice.

'I've no idea. Try to look at it from my point of view. Here is this young girl, seemingly stabbed to death, and being examined, superficially, by two local doctors. I arrive, a stranger, and they are naturally on their guard in case I criticise anything they've done. And I am equally on my guard, to be sure I don't. So far as they're concerned, the girl died from a stab wound. They would think I was several kinds of a fool if I started making internal examinations. Besides which, it would arouse their curiosity, and you and I know that's always a bad thing.'

'You're right of course. I need hardly tell you doctor, I shall be waiting for your findings with even more impatience than usual.'

Whatmore grinned.

'I'll bet. I won't delay any longer than is absolutely necessary.'

Then a further thought occurred to the superintendent.

'Have they told you about this boy, Benson?'

'No. Who's he?'

'Boy friend.'

Vine went on to explain the background, which had led up to the young man's death in the car-smash. Vine listened carefully.

'Is he down at the morgue?'

'Yes, he is. You see, doctor, on the face of it, we had a rather straightforward case of young lovers falling out. The boy lost his temper, and struck out. The girl died. It wasn't quite that simple of course, one or two bits to be explained. But that was the general picture. What you're telling me now—'

'—suggesting now—'

'—all right, suggesting now, could put an entirely different complexion on the whole series of events. Young chaps who lose their tempers don't carry bottles of poison around, in case they do. Poison means planning, and planning means premeditation.'

That was too self-evident to call for comment.

'Boyfriend, though. Could account for the love bite.'

39

'Yes. But this other factor you mentioned. Is it possible to tell, by examining Benson's body, whether he had intercourse just before he died? Or tried to?'

'I can do that. And it certainly seems necessary. Because if he didn't—'

'—if he didn't, we have, as our American friends would say, a whole new ball-game.'

He sounded so despondent that Whatmore chuckled.

'Never despair, superintendent. It's only three thirty in the morning. Lots to do yet, before breakfast.'

'Too true. Well, we'd better get back inside, and get on with it.'

In the changing room, Vine took a last look at the girl. The eyes had bothered him before, but that was chiefly because of the naked terror they showed. Now, he was thinking something else. If the arrow thrust had caused her death, surely the eyes would have shown pain? Some dreadful anguish would have been reflected? Not being a medical man, he couldn't be sure. But, if the doctor was right, if death had occurred before the blow, then perhaps there had been no pain. Only terror as to what was about to happen to her, whatever it was. It was a possibility.

He left the doctors with their emergency arrangements for transporting Elizabeth Warren off to the mortuary, and went in search of Inspector Cornwell.

40

The inspector had been spending his time reassuring the waiting guests that they would not be detained very much longer. His own relief at the return of his superior was visible.

'All ready to start, inspector?'

'Whenever you say, sir.'

'Right. In here, first.'

Inside the room, Vine looked at Cornwell hard.

'Small shift of emphasis, inspector. I am particularly anxious to pinpoint any pieces of evidence which may help to prove that this crime was committed by someone other than young Benson. And, if possible, to find out who that other person might be.'

The inspector felt offended. It was almost as if his superior was suggesting that any such evidence might previously have been overlooked. As if there was some intention on his part to point the finger at Benson.

'Naturally, sir, I would have hoped proper account would have been taken of all available evidence in any case.'

'And you would be right, inspector. It would be. Don't get huffy. What I'm saying is, we're going to push people, and keep on pushing, until they remember the tiniest detail. Not just such general background as will fit the facts we have. It's very easy, and sometimes tempting, in a situation like this, to go for a nice obvious solution. If you have to skate over one or two factors that don't seem to fit perfectly, well, that's life. Only we're not going to skate over them. We're going to polish them up, enlarge them, add to them if we can. If, at the end, we put the blame on the deceased Benson, it's going to be because he's guilty. Not just because he's there. Do I make myself clear?'

'Perfectly clear, sir.'

'Good. Then let's have the first customer.'

*   *   *

At five twenty a.m., Superintendent Vine leaned back, yawned, and scratched at his head.

'Lord, I'm tired. How many left?'

'Just one sir. The caretaker, George Spinks. I kept him till the end because he lives here, anyway. He can't lock up till we've finished.'

'That's the chap who met me when I came in?'

'Yes sir.'

Vine's eyes gleamed.

'Was he on the door all night?'

'He acted as a sort of doorman and ticket-checker, yes. He always does when the club has a function.'

'Then, assuming he came through the front door, and not straight up from the gates of hell, as some of these people seem to think, this weirdo will have been seen by Spinks face to face.'

Cornwell nodded.

'That would be correct, sir. Unless he sneaked in.'

His superior turned back over his notes.

'I was looking for that fourth witness, chap with the steel specs.'

'Mr. Adams, sir.'

'That's him. Tell me what your notes say. I thought his account about this nutcase was the most interesting. He was the only one who was certain about the chap's name, for a start.'

The inspector began to read.

'Witness number four. Reginald Adams, age twenty seven, occupation librarian.'

Reg Adams had sat, looking at the two police officers, and waiting. The older one spoke first.

'Sorry to have kept you so long, Mr. Adams, but I'm sure you will appreciate the gravity of the position.'

'Oh, I quite understand.'

'The inspector tells me that shortly after he arrived here, you told him you had information which might be valuable. Is that correct?'

Adams nodded, but without enthusiasm. What had seemed of enormous importance in the excitement of the moment had shrunk noticeably as the cold hours of the night wore on. Particularly now, when everybody thought Tony Benson had killed Liz. His little bit of news no longer seemed very interesting.

'Well, Mr. Adams?' prompted the inspector.

43

He swallowed. Might as well get it over with.

'Probably nothing, I can see that now.'

'We'd like to hear it, though.'

'Well, it was about that chap, the one who called himself Nosferatu.'

The two officers exchanged glances.

'Are you sure about the name, sir? None of the other witnesses seems at all clear about that.' He looked surprised.

'Can't think why. He said it loud enough. And clearly enough, I would have thought.'

Vine felt a familiar quickening of interest.

'An unusual name, though. Odd that you should be so positive.'

'Not a bit. Anyone who knows the first thing about movies would recognise it at once.'

The superintendent leaned back. He was about to learn something, and he could feel it.

'I don't know the first thing about movies Mr. Adams, and I'm sure the inspector is the same. Won't you enlighten us?'

Adams removed his glasses and began to polish at them.

'I'm something of a buff, you might say. Enthusiastic amateur, you know. As soon as this character said he was Nosferatu, I began to listen very hard. You see, that is the title of the first great vampire film. It was made in Germany, in 1922, by Felix Murnau. Dracula was played by Max Schreck. Of course, they didn't call him Dracula, they called him Count

Orlock, probably so as to avoid infringement of copyright or something, but that's who the character was supposed to be, just the same. And then, when he went on to say he was from the Council of the Undead, well, that was just icing on the cake.'

'I see. It is obvious that you are an expert, Mr. Adams,' Vine assured him smoothly. 'Please tell us more.'

'More?'

'Yes, about this Dracula business.'

Adams shook his head.

'Wrong man, I'm afraid. All I know is what I see on the screen. I don't know anything about Dracula as a subject. You want to talk to Colin James. I was pulling his leg last night, but he got a bit huffy. Not a laughing matter, for him.'

'Is Mr. James here now?' asked Cornwell quickly.

'Don't think so. Spent most of his time in the bar, you see. I fancy one of your men will have his address.'

The inspector prayed silently that it might be so. 'You can't help us there?'

''Fraid not. He lives in South Town somewhere, but I couldn't give the actual address.'

Superintendent Vine broke in.

'There's no hurry. Tomorrow will do. Thank you for your help, Mr. Adams. It's been most enlightening.'

Inspector Cornwell was able to reconstruct

most of this conversation from his notes. When he reached the end, he looked over at his superior.

'That's all I have, sir.'

'Much the same as me,' confirmed Vine. 'All right, let's have a look at Mr. Spinks, see what he's got to say.'

George Spinks sat down wearily. What these people didn't seem to realise was that he would have at least an hour's work to do after they'd all gone. Then the secretary expected the place to open up again at nine o'clock, just as though nothing had happened. Well we'd see about that, we would. People could muck George Spinks about just so far, and then they'd find he wasn't so easy. By no means. We'd see about that.

In answer to the inspector's question, he confirmed that he'd been on duty at the entrance from the outset.

'And more than an hour before. These things don't arrange themselves, you know.'

'Quite. And you obviously did a first-class job, Mr. Spinks. Most successful. Now were you at the door when this stranger arrived?'

'You mean the head-case? Chap who put the screamers up everybody?'

Vine hid a grin by lighting a fresh cigarette. Cornwell carried on with his questioning.

'Yes, that sounds like him. Could you tell us what happened? Every little detail that you can remember.'

George coughed importantly.

'Yes, well, let's see. He came in, and I asked him if he was the conjuror. That annoyed him, for a start. Asked if that was my idea of a joke.'

'Why should he think that?'

'I dunno. Unusual name of course, but nothing funny that I can see.'

'Name?' Vine interrupted suddenly. 'You didn't say anything about a name.'

'Yes I did,' retorted George. 'I just told you. I said to him "Are you Mr. Le Fanu?" That's when he turned nasty.'

Vine pressed the point.

'He seemed to be upset by the name, not the fact that you mistook him for a magician?'

'That's what I said.'

Really, thought George, you have to tell some people the same thing ten times over.

'Go on, Mr. Spinks. What happened next? Did he have a ticket?'

'Oh yes, proper ticket. Tell you the truth inspector, he was such a queer looking geyser, I asked him who he was.'

'And did he tell you?'

'He told me, all right. Told me to mind me own business. To be quite honest, he had every right, you know. As long as people had proper tickets, it wasn't up to me to ask who they were.'

Cornwell smiled sympathetically.

'I can understand that. You were probably a bit rattled, and the question just popped out.'

47

'That's it, yes.'

Reasonable fellow, this inspector. Not too sure about his boss.

'And that's all that happened? No other conversation, no incident that occurred?'

'No. Mind you, there was an incident, but that was inside. You don't see much of the fun when you're on the door.'

The inspector looked at Vine, who shook his head. George Spinks was allowed to go.

'What do you make of that, inspector?'

'Nothing much, sir. The ticket, of course. Like to know where he bought that.'

'Mr. Beamish is probably still around. Go and tackle him about it. Oh, and see if you can wangle me some more coffee, will you?'

'Will do.'

Vine sat back, with his eyes closed. A stranger would have assumed he was taking forty winks. Anybody who knew him would recognise a favourite thinking posture. At that moment, he was thinking back over everything he'd been told in the past couple of hours, everything he'd seen.

The door opened and Inspector Cornwell returned, carrying two cups of coffee and pushing the door closed with his foot.

'Ah. I always think that a copper who can track down coffee at ten to six in the morning ought to be able to cope with a simple case of murder.'

'There we are, sir. And it's hot. Now about

48

those tickets. They were distributed on a businesslike basis, certain shops in the town, certain committee members, and so on, a proper list was kept, of who had which numbers, who had paid, and so forth. I've been through the returns with Mr. Beamish, and I think we may have something.'

Cornwell could not conceal his pleasure. The superintendent stirred at his coffee, and said slowly, 'Let me have a little guess, inspector. Shot in the dark. No penalties if I'm wrong.'

'Of course, sir.'

'One member bought two tickets, but didn't bring a partner. The member was Mr. Colin James.'

Cornwell's face fell, and Vine chuckled.

'But how did you—I mean, how could you possibly—'

'Know? I didn't. It was a real shot in the dark, as I said. If you get enough of them right, over the years, you get promoted. Mr. James is beginning to sound like a very interesting chap, wouldn't you say?'

'I would sir, I would indeed.'

The inspector was still floundering in his own disappointment, at having his big surprise forestalled.

'Had he left his address?'

'No need, sir. I got it from the club records, anyway.'

'Well then, finish your coffee, and we'll go

and have a little chat with him.'

Cornwell looked at his watch.

'What, at six o'clock in the morning, sir? He won't have been in bed more than two or three hours.'

'Yes, at six o'clock in the morning, sir,' mimicked his superior. 'As for his sleep, he's had more than I've had. And you've had none at all. Think of that young girl out there. Think how delighted her family would be, if she could be woken up by a couple of rude coppers. But she won't be, inspector. She's been murdered. I want to trace this Nos—what's it—'

'Nosferatu.'

'—Nosferatu. And quick. Maybe he knows something, and maybe he doesn't, but I've got to be satisfied about that. Where are you going?'

Cornwell was halfway to the door.

'To tell my sergeant to ensure the murder area is kept under watch, until you say otherwise.'

'Right. It'll be light in a couple of hours. We'll be back by then. Unless we're fighting Satan in some dark alley.'

He began to pack his slim briefcase.

CHAPTER FOUR

Colin James lived in a tree-lined avenue to the south of the town. The houses were large, solid structures, with gardens front and rear, and here and there an ornamental pond to grace the approach.

'Nice area,' grunted the superintendent. 'Not many P.C.s living down here, I shouldn't wonder.'

'Nor inspectors sir,' agreed Cornwell, adding privately 'or superintendents, for that matter'.

They located the house easily enough, and parked outside the front door. The door was answered at the first pushing of the bell, and they were confronted by a large grey-haired man in a dressing gown.

'We are police officers, sir,' announced Vine. 'We would like to see Mr. Colin James, if he's here.'

'Here? Well, of course he's here. It's his home,' grunted the householder. 'Anyway, this is a hell of a time to call. What's it all about?'

'I'm sorry, but I prefer to discuss that with Mr. James.'

'I'm his father, and this is my house.'

Vine sighed.

'And your son is twenty four years old, not a child, Mr. James. Would you tell him we're here, please.'

'You'd better come in, I suppose.' James Senior stood to one side, to allow them entry into the hall. 'Damned inconsiderate. Chap's only been home since three o'clock.'

'We appreciate that, sir. Believe me, we wouldn't disturb him if it wasn't necessary.'

'H'mph.'

Mr. James stomped up the stairs, muttering. The two policemen exchanged glances, but said nothing. Instead, they took in the gloomy hall, with its ancient grandfather clock, and a rubber tree yearning for the Malayan air. After some murmuring upstairs, James Senior came back down.

'Go on up, will you? Second door on the right. He's just getting a dressing gown on.'

'Thank you, sir.'

They went up the wide stairway side by side, pausing at the second door, and knocking.

'Just a minute. Hang on.' Then, 'O.K. Come in.'

Vine led the way into a bedroom cum living room. The bed was a narrow divan, which was obviously turned into a couch during the day. On this, half-asleep and rubbing at his face, sat a sallow-faced young man.

'Mr. Colin James? We are police officers.'

The young man nodded. He didn't seem very surprised, nor, for that matter, especially interested.

'Take a pew,' he waved. 'Want some

52

coffee?'

'If it isn't too much trouble, Mr. James. Very kind of you.'

'No trouble,' he assured them. 'Have to be mugs, though. My ma won't trust me with cups and saucers.'

He switched on a waiting kettle, and removed earthenware mugs from a bedside cupboard.

'I suppose you've come about poor Liz,' he continued. 'Well, what can I do to help?'

His back was to the seated men. Cornwell indicated with his eyes towards the far corner of the room. A devil mask was mounted on the wall, above a pair of crossed daggers, and below a faded yellow parchment, which was stretched lengthwise, and securely fastened to prevent it snapping back into a scroll.

'Was the—was Miss Warren a close friend of yours, sir?'

'Close? No. I've played tennis with her a few times, but that's all. She's—she was—Tony's girl. Tony Benson, but I expect you know all that.'

Vine ignored this.

'A terrible tragedy altogether,' he went on, 'and in such a macabre setting. I may tell you sir, in all my years on the force, I've never known anything quite so bizarre.'

James said nothing, but both men noted the sudden tightening of his grip on the milkbottle he was holding.

'We're just trying to sketch in all the background, Mr. James. Would you mind telling us what costume you wore last night?'

'Costume? None. Not a proper one, that is. Just a dinner jacket with an old-fashioned sort of ruff affair. Kind of poor imitation Regency buck.'

'Quite understand,' commented Vine equably. 'Don't care much for fancy dress myself.'

'It isn't that, at all,' said James, suddenly vehement. 'It's—'

His voice died away, and he stirred instant coffee into boiling water with vigour.

'It's what, sir?'

'Nothing,' he replied quietly.

'Oh come, sir, must be something. You were saying that you didn't really object to ordinary fancy dress, but last night was different.'

'Did I say that?' The young man's voice was confused.

'You did, sir. Were you going on to say that it struck you as wrong, the way people dressed up last night? A blasphemy, perhaps?'

The last words were shot out staccato, like machine-gun bullets.

'Well, that's what it was, wasn't it? Mockery of Him and His angels, His disciples. Call it what you will.'

Inspector Cornwell was shocked at the change in that sallow face. The eyes had begun to burn with a strange brightness, and the lower jaw was working convulsively.

There was nothing in the superintendent's tone to indicate that he had noticed anything unusual. 'That coffee looks good, Mr. James. May I?'

'Eh? Oh yes. Of course.'

Colin James handed over the steaming mugs, then sat down heavily on the bed, nursing his own coffee. Vine spoke again.

'You know, it's been my experience that people shouldn't meddle with things they don't understand. I think we're agreed on that?'

'Completely. I told them, you know. Told the committee, when they first floated this ghastly scheme. They took no notice, of course.'

'People seldom do. And there was nothing you could have done to prevent it. I'm sure you would have done what you could.'

James nodded quickly.

'Oh yes, I did. Naturally I did. I went to everyone I know. But do you know something strange?'

'Yes, I think I do. These people, who profess to follow the one true faith, they declined to come forward publicly. Am I right?'

'Completely. Oh, completely. I was horrified. I mean here was this stupid and dangerous affair about to be held, and the very people who should have been in the forefront, shouting it down, they wouldn't lift a finger. I was getting quite desperate.'

Vine nodded.

'Understandable. You were afraid of what offence might be given to the powers of darkness, and of what retribution they might exact.'

Inspector Cornwell was beginning partly to understand the conversation, but it was a slow process.

'Tell me Mr. James, how did you come to contact Mr. Nosferatu?'

The question was put quite casually, and prompted a reply in the same offhand fashion.

'Well, I'd heard of him, but I didn't actually know the man. If I'm to be perfectly open with you, I must say I think these vampire people are not to be taken very seriously. I know they mean well, and all that, but the whole cult seems to me to be something of a sideshow. They are more concerned with the paraphernalia, the rituals, of what is after all no more than an offshoot of the main culture. Spending time which ought to be devoted to the study of the true understanding of Evil. Stop me, if I go on a bit, but this is something of a talking point with me.'

He looked at the superintendent with concern, as though anxious not to be wasting everyone's time. Not that he needed to worry about that, reflected Cornwell. Mr. James Junior was doing fine.

'I understand your view on that, sir, but

nevertheless you did contact this man eventually.'

It was not a question, but a statement of fact.

'Yes. I got in touch with him, and explained what was happening here. He was very shocked, and agreed at once that he would do what he could.'

'So you obtained a ticket for him,' Vine contributed. 'Tell me, did you post it, or did he collect it from you?'

The question seemed so unimportant that James looked surprised.

'I posted it. What's the difference?'

'The difference is, sir, that you have the gentleman's address. Could I trouble you for that, please?'

The young man looked doubtful.

'Don't know about that. Handing out a chap's address, you know, and without his permission.'

'Quite understand, sir. But this is not a casual enquiry. It is a case of murder. The murder of one of your own friends. If you insist on my going through official channels of course—'

'—no. I see what you mean. This is no time to be delicate. It's around here somewhere.'

He rummaged round in a drawer, finding a small notebook, and riffling through the pages.

'Here we are. Like me to copy it out?'

'Thank you.'

With the address in his pocket, the superintendent rose.

'You've been very helpful, Mr. James. One last favour, if you wouldn't mind. It would not help us if you were to advise Mr. Nosferatu that we were coming to see him.'

Colin James looked offended.

'Do you mean tip him off?' he queried. 'You seem to think I belong to some underworld syndicate or something.'

Vine's face was very serious when he replied.

'Nothing of the kind, sir. On the contrary, I'm sure you lead an entirely blameless life. I don't think we shall be troubling you again in this connection. My advice would be for you to keep out of it. You know how it is. Small town, this. The newspapers will be having some fun with the case, you can rely on it. No reason for your name ever to be mentioned, as far as we're concerned. But, of course, I can't tell you what to do.'

The young face was relieved.

'Yes. I see what you mean. Don't worry, I shan't do anything to draw attention to myself.'

Downstairs, they found James Senior walking slowly up and down. He looked at them anxiously.

'Look here, there's no trouble, is there? My boy—'

'Your boy is perfectly all right, sir,' Vine

58

assured him. 'He's just been helping us on a couple of points.'

'His mother, you see. Sick woman. She couldn't—'

'Perfectly all right,' repeated the superintendent. 'No need for the lady to be troubled. Come to that, there's no need for her ever to know we came. We shan't be bothering Colin again.'

The relief on the man's face was vivid.

'Thank God.'

Outside, they got into the car.

'Back to the club, sir?'

'Yes. I'll get through to the Met. boys. See if they have anything on this chap Nosferatu. Fancy a day in the Smoke, inspector?'

'Make a nice change, sir.'

'M'm. What did you think of young James?' Cornwell pulled out to avoid a milk float emerging from a side lane.

'Harmless, I would have said. Mucking about with Devil worship. He can't know much about it, or be seriously involved. If he was, he wouldn't have let you con him quite so easily. He'd have shut up like a clam. As it was, you had him burbling away like a professional grass.'

Vine looked at his junior out of the corner of his eye. He wasn't certain that what he considered the adroit and guileless way he'd led the witness ought to be dismissed as 'conning'. Still, he admitted, it had been rather

59

easy.

'Shouldn't write him off too easily,' he said. 'If you start finding disembowelled chickens around the patch, keep him in mind.'

'Will do.'

It was almost full daylight when they arrived back at the club.

'I'll put that call in to the Met. first,' announced Vine, as they walked in. 'Then I'll have a look at the scene of the crime. Hallo, watch your tongue.'

Two men stood talking with the uniformed officer guarding the door. One was in his early twenties. The other was forty-odd, with a grim face and hands plunged deep in the pockets of a battered trench coat.

'Mr. Vine, isn't it?' greeted the young one. 'I know Inspector Cornwell, naturally. Andy Chivers, Great Bravington Chronicle and Gazette.'

Vine acknowledged this with a brief nod, then looked enquiringly at the older man.

'Bill Wallington,' he announced. 'From the other one.

'The other one?' repeated Vine, puzzled.

'The other Chronicle. The Daily one.'

The national press. This quickly. The superintendent frowned.

'Gentlemen, I have an urgent call to make. As soon as it's done, I'll give you a statement. Say half an hour.'

'Who's this call to?' queried Wallington.

60

'Half an hour,' repeated Vine, firmly.

'The public are entitled—' began the reporter.

'To as much information as I can release, without prejudicing my enquiries. And they will have it. In thirty minutes.'

The two police officers went into the club.

'Bit sharp off the mark, that chap from the Chronicle,' observed Cornwell.

'I know what's happened,' growled Vine. 'One of the lovely guests thought he might pick up a quick tenner if he phoned in. Oh Lord, what is it now?'

A constable was waiting to speak to them.

'Excuse me sir, there's a man waiting to see you. Don't know how he got inside. Rum sort of bloke. Says it's important.'

'Oh. Did he give a name?'

The constable produced his notebook.

'Queer name, sir. Had to write it down. Sort of foreign. Yes, here it is. Mr. Nosferatu.'

The two senior officers looked at each other.

'Well, well,' muttered the superintendent. 'Let's not keep him waiting.'

CHAPTER FIVE

As experienced police officers, both men had applied a percentage of mental discount to the

61

descriptions given of the intruder at the Horror Ball. All were supplied by people under a certain amount of stress. There had been a murder of someone they knew, there had been a goodly consumption of the so-called Transylvanian wine, and it was, in addition, a bizarre setting.

They had noted words like 'Spectre', 'ghoul', and 'corpse-like'. Noted them carefully down, deciding quietly that this chap must have outdone most of the guests in his attempts at a ghastly appearance. That, and no more.

When they saw the figure that rose as they entered the room, they were both taken considerably aback. The man, if it was a man, really did chill the blood. It was as though some damnable image from a nightmare had survived into the daylight hours.

Vine was the first to recover his composure.

'Mr. Nosferatu?' he asked, formally.

'Nosferatu is title and name in one,' returned the other. His voice had a dry hissing to it.

'Quite. My name is Vine, Superintendent Vine, and this is Inspector Cornwell.'

The visitor inclined his head. Dammit, he really was corpse-like, decided the inspector.

'Please sit down, Mr., er, that is, Nosferatu. Good of you to come. I had been hoping to ask you some questions.'

'My aim is to assist you. That is why I am

here.'

For the next quarter of an hour, they subjected him to a thorough examination about the events of the night before. He submitted to it all with an icy detachment which was unsettling. The account of the night's events which emerged was in every way a corroboration of what they had been told by most of the other witnesses. It was confined to his own participation, since he could contribute nothing about what happened after his ejection from the premises. Outside, he had walked through the surrounding country, communing, to quote his own words, with the creatures of the night. He had seen and heard nothing of any help to them concerning the actual murder.

Vine was puzzled. Here was this man, confirming with every reply that he was ready-made for the role of chief suspect, and yet doing so almost with condescension. It was as if he were royalty, humouring the locals over their little rituals.

'You must understand,' said Vine heavily, 'that your replies are putting you in a vulnerable position. On your own admission, you were alone out there in the night. Free to do as you wished, and with no witness.'

Nosferatu received this with disdain, then dismissed it.

'I am here to help you, not to listen to your infantile mental stumblings. There is a madman to be caught, and it is important that he be caught quickly.'

The superintendent swallowed.

'Why is it important to you?' he demanded.

'He blasphemes.'

The two policemen looked at each other.

'Could you explain that a bit?'

Bony fingers stabbed at them from a scarecrow arm.

'You are thinking of this as some sordid murder, just like any other. You are wrong. I warned them here last night of the dangers, but they would not listen. So be it. Perhaps, now that my words have been proved, perhaps you will.'

'Any information you can give us—' began Vine, but the other was not listening.

'What took place here was a ritual. Some tormented creature was here, someone who deludes himself, thinks of himself as that which he is not. He must be found, and stopped.'

'Found, yes. But you say stopped. As though he might be going to strike again. What makes you say that? And what do you mean, when you say he thinks he is something he isn't?'

The glowing eyes focussed on a point in the middle distance.

'I came here, to this place, because I feared these idiots might offend against the Great One. I feared that in His wrath, He might wreak some terrible vengeance against them.

64

They are but children, babbling cretins. They are unworthy of His anger.'

Cornwell shifted uncomfortably in his seat. His superior shot him a warning look.

'Why should it matter to you?' demanded Vine.

The burning glance raked across his face.

'Because the time is not yet,' intoned Nosferatu. 'It is too soon. We prepare, we make ready, as we have all these years. The Master waits. He knows of our work. Knows of me, Nosferatu, His true disciple. When the Day of Blackness comes, I shall summon Him forth to His rightful kingdom. The kingdom of Earth.'

The eyes were now like fiery coals in that death-mask face. Both the listeners felt their own strength being sapped away under the dominating presence of evil. It was cold in the room.

It was Vine who pulled himself together first, rising to his feet with a snort.

'Look here, this is all very interesting, but I'm investigating a case of murder. Straightforward murder. None of this stuff about the powers of darkness comes into it at all.'

Cornwell shook his head, to dispel the encroaching lethargy.

'You are wrong, policeman.'

The judgement was issued in a flat, detached voice.

'Convince me,' offered Vine. 'You said yourself this is the work of a madman.'

'That is correct. But, a particular kind of madman. One who thinks himself that which he is not. A blasphemer.'

'That's the second time you've said that,' pointed out the superintendent. 'Mind telling me what you mean?'

'The man thinks himself a reincarnation.'

'How can you possibly know what he thinks?'

'You have seen the evidence.' Nosferatu's tone was becoming impatient. 'The bite at the neck, the stake through the heart. The madman thinks—forgive me, Master—the man thinks he is Vlad.'

'Vlad?'

Vine looked at the inspector, whose face was equally puzzled. They both betrayed mild alarm when Nosferatu rose to his feet. Power seemed to radiate from that withered frame.

'Vlad Tepes,' and his voice carried chill penetration, 'Vlad the Impaler, Son of Dracul.'

'Dracul,' repeated the superintendent, 'Son of Dracul. That would be—'

'—Dracula,' whispered the horrified Cornwell.

Outside, a dog howled. Then another.

Nosferatu had fallen to his knees, head bowed, and was muttering rapidly in a language neither man could identify. Vine

66

jerked his head towards the door, and Cornwell was glad to follow him into the corridor.

'This chap ought to be certified,' breathed Vine.

'Quite agree, sir. Just the same—'

'Well?'

'I'm wondering whether he might be on to something, I don't know much about this Dracula. Saw a film once, that's about all. But he was supposed to bite necks, to draw the blood. There was something about a wooden stake, as well. But I thought that was used to kill the vampire, not the victim. I could be wrong.'

The superintendent barked.

'I think we've let this bloke get too much of a hold on us. I know he's a spooky character, and so on, but I've got a murder investigation to get on with. Get his statement written down, inspector, cutting out all the mystic rubbish, and join me outside.'

'Right, sir.'

Cornwell opened the door, and went back inside. Two seconds later, he was running after the superintendent.

'Sir, sir.'

Vine waited for him to catch up.

'Well?'

'He's gone, sir. No sign of him.'

'There was an outside door, man. Get after him, he can't get far.'

67

But there was nothing to be found of Nosferatu. No one had seen him go. No car had left the car park. Superintendent Vine was annoyed, but no more.

Inspector Cornwell was decidedly uneasy.

*   *   *

Bill Wallington had grown tired of waiting outside the entrance. Leaving the local reporter to hold the fort, he strolled around the outside of the clubhouse. Peering in at the windows, he was able to build a good picture of what it must have looked like at the height of the festivities. He began to rehearse phrases in his mind, good reliable stuff for the breakfast table. Pity there couldn't be any pictures of the guests in their rigouts. A couple of monsters and a werewolf or two would have made a lovely layout.

'Here, what're you up to?'

He turned at the complaining voice, and saw an elderly man watching him with suspicion. Maybe the old boy would know something.

'Wallington, Daily Chronicle.' He pulled out his press card, and held it for his questioner to see. 'Important story, this. National coverage. I expect it will be on the front page. You'll be able to read about what happened, Mr—?'

'Spinks. George Spinks. And I don't need to read what happened, thank you very much. I know more about it than anybody.'

The reporter congratulated himself. This could be good.

'Mr Spinks?' he repeated. 'Why, of course, I've heard your name already. You seem to have been in the thick of it.'

George straightened his shoulders.

'It was me let him in,' he announced importantly.

'Let him in?' echoed Wallington vaguely.

'Him what done it. The murderer. Butcher, more like.'

'I see,' and the man from Fleet Street was impressed. George could tell by his tone. 'What sort of man was he?'

The caretaker harrumphed.

'Man? Well I've been thinking about that. Wondering if he was really a man at all. Them eyes. Bore holes in your face, they could. And the rest of him, well. I tell you, Mr. Warrington—'

'—Wallington—'

'—sorry, I tell you, if you'd took a skeleton from the grave, and put a suit of clothes on it, you'd have got something more human-looking than him.'

Of course, Wallington realised. The costume party. This man must have taken more trouble than the others. His interest began to fade.

'Really looked the part, did he?'

George was offended.

'Looked the part? No, he did not. The bloke was the real thing. Put the fear of death into me. And everybody in there,' nodding inside the club. 'Put the shivers right up 'em. Stopped the whole dance, he did. They had to throw him out. Came and helped me guard the entrance, to stop him getting in again. Course, we wasn't to know. He wasn't coming back. He was out there somewhere, murdering that poor little girl.'

Wallington took out his notebook.

'Tell me a bit more, Mr. Spinks. Tell me about when you first saw him.'

Ten minutes later, he was still scribbling furiously.

'And did you actually see the body?'

'Not when they brought her in. I was at the front you see. But I went round the back when I heard.'

Morbid old bugger.

'The report I had said she was stabbed. Was the knife still in the body?'

'Knife? There wasn't no knife. Arrow, she was done with. Stuck right through her, right through her poor heart.'

Wallington's pencil stopped moving.

'An arrow?' he queried. 'Are you sure about that?'

'Course I'm sure. Played enough bows and arrows when I was a boy. Ought to know one when I see one.'

They were interrupted by a new voice.

'Oh, there you are, Mr. Spinks. Wanted inside, please.'

A police officer was beckoning from a corner of the building. George Spinks nodded importantly.

'That'll be the superintendent, I expect. Key witness, you see. Told you I was.'

'Thank you very much,' nodded Wallington. 'Perhaps we can talk again later.'

The caretaker bustled officiously away. Wallington stared down at his notes.

Arrow. A very nice change indeed. Should be able to make something out of that. Robin Hood? The Robin Hood murder? No. That wouldn't do. Thief and murderer that he was, he was still a good guy in the public image. To call this killer Robin Hood was almost certain to get him an acquittal before they even caught him. William Tell? No. Another good guy. Arrow. Archery. The Midnight Archer? Even as he thought it, a familiar theme tune came into his mind, and he grinned. The Midnight Archers, an every night story of country murders. What about historic arrows? King Harold's eyes. Achilles' heel. No. Too obscure.

The horror angle, then.

Frankenstein, Dracula, the Wolf Man. Vampires, ghouls—vampires. He looked back at his notes quickly. What was that magician's name again? Le Fanu the Magnificent. Le Fanu. That was familiar, surely? There was an author by that name, long dead. Sheridan Le

Fanu, something like that. Easily look it up. He had written one of the great vampire classics, Wallington was sure of it. Didn't help much though. Vampires didn't use arrows. You didn't kill them with arrows either. You had to have—what was it—a silver bullet? Or—he almost snapped the pencil as it struck him.

Or a wooden stake through the heart.

He'd got it. A real eye-catcher. Something to bring the chill of the grave wafting over the cornflakes.

The masked ball. The ghastly intruder. The body of the young virgin, pierced by a deadly wooden stake.

The headline shrieked at him from his scribbled notes.

The Dracula Murder.

CHAPTER SIX

Three days later, Bill Wallington stood in the saloon bar of the Feathers, staring moodily at the last inch of beer in his glass. It was a few minutes past ten thirty in the morning, and this was already his second pint.

'Hallo Bill. Want one in there?'

He looked up as Bertie Renouf of the Globe leaned next to him.

'Hallo, Bertie. No. I'll have to go back in a minute. Bit of typing.'

The other man nodded.

'Half of Guinness, Bas. Thought you were doing this civic corruption story? Frank is still up there.'

'Got fed up with it. Same old garbage. Bunch of grubby little councillors with their fingers in the till. Rolls Royce on the rates. Boozing parties every other day. Exhibitions at the local whore-shop. They make me sick. They're so bloody venal, these types. Crooked as hell, every chance to make it pay, and can't get their minds higher than their bellies. Nasty little planning permissions, fifty quid here, a hundred there. Wouldn't be so bad if they were ambitious. Flog the town hall to a supermarket chain. Something big. I don't have to be there. As long as I can spell the names right, I can write the story out of my head.'

Renouf nodded, sipping at his Guinness.

'Nice drop of beer. Cold. Bas always keeps it nice and cold.'

Poor old Bill, he did look fed up. He must have had a terrible roasting over that Dracula story he did. Everybody else played it fairly straight, but the Chronicle had gone steaming away with this crazy vampire theme. Sold a few newspapers, but made themselves look very silly when it turned out the girl had been poisoned. Nasty enough, mind you. A small scratch inside the wrist had been sufficient to introduce some virulent poison into the bloodstream, and the girl had died in less than a minute. If they'd found that scratch before Wallington got his vampires on the wing, the Chronicle might have had time to scrub the story. As it was, every other national had called it the clubhouse Drama, or Horror Ball brings Horror. Nobody else had included six hundred words on twentieth century vampirism. Wallington was still smarting from the news editor's tongue. And from being sent out to cover some second-rate story of municipal fiddling.

'Mr. Wallington.'

A small sharp-faced man poked his head into the bar.

'Wanted Mr. Wallington.'

'All right, Tiny. Tell him I'll be there in a minute.'

'Don't recommend it. ' 'E's looking like one of his moods. If you want to upset him, that's up to you. But don't ask me to do it for you.'

Wallington scowled, and emptied his glass.

'All right Tiny don't nag. D'you know, in another incarnation, you would have been an agent for a press gang.'

Tiny chuckled.

'That's what this is though, innit? A press gang.'

'Oh Christ. Well, I suppose I asked for it. Lead on McTiny.'

*   *   *

74

No one could say the people who ran the Crypt were believers in harsh lighting. The light was so poor that you could easily bump into a chair or a table when you first came in, and before your eyes adjusted to the gloom. It all went to provide what the management called an intimate atmosphere. You couldn't see people three yards away. You couldn't see what you were drinking. And especially you couldn't see any telltale signs on the girls' faces. Like crowsfeet, lines, extra chins, and other little time-ravages that showed all too soon under more conventional lighting.

The police weren't too happy about The Crypt. Sooner or later they would have to crack down on it, but for the moment it was safe. It was, after all, only three months since it had been closed down. On that occasion it had been the Captain's Cabin. The time before, the sign outside announced it as Miss Ella's Joint. But too many of the male customers had thought the other males were cabin boys, in the one case. And too many of both sexes were smoking Miss Ella's joints, in the other.

The latest letting was as The Crypt, the place with the intimate atmosphere. It provided the ladies of the night with a place to sit down for half an hour, and perhaps find a new friend for another half-hour. Longer, if he could afford it. And it provided a useful touch of glamorous night-life for hotel receptionists to whisper behind their hands to the overnight conference crowd. If a man felt the need to pay the two pounds entrance charge, plus another two for a glass of watered scotch, then it was the solemn duty of the management of The Crypt to make these facilities available.

Behind the bar, the giant figure of Jo-Jo dispensed drinks with calm disapproval, and watched out for any opportunity to use his enormous physical strength against anyone disturbing the peace of his domain.

'Ginger ale, Jo-Jo.'

A new arrival, a dark-haired woman who could have been twenty, or forty, slapped coins on the counter. Jo-Jo slopped the drink anyhow into a glass, and slid it in front of her.

'Gentleman, you are. A real gent. I always say that.'

He pulled his arm sideways across his face, in a threatening gesture, and she moved away. At a corner table sat two other women.

'Hi.'

The newcomer sat down with them. They noted her arrival without much interest.

'Busy, is it?'

'Not much. Early yet.'

'Still. Better in here than out in that bleeding fog.'

'You're right Edie.'

Edie sipped at the ginger ale.

'No ice,' she complained. 'Mean bugger. Honest, he treats us like dirt, that Jo Jo.'

One of the others nodded abstractedly.

'Not his type, are we? Likes little boys. You've seen him acting up, if we get a few of those-student-types in.'

'Gawd yes. Like a virgin at a wedding, isn't he? Makes you sick.'

The third woman had kept silent, but now she spoke.

'Unnatural, that's what it is. Unnatural.'

Edie nodded.

'Haven't seen Irish Mollie have you, Sandra? Said she'd be in Fat Jack's at ten o'clock, but she never showed up.'

Sandra lit a cigarette.

'She's got a chump. Good for a couple of hours, if you ask me.'

'Right,' agreed the third one. 'He didn't get that suit down the market.'

Edie clucked her tongue.

'I hope not. We're doing a double act at twelve o'clock. Race course people. Nice classy job. Don't want to turn up on me own. When did she glue on to this mark?'

'I'm not a bleeding timekeeper,' Sandra replied. 'Bout half an hour ago, I suppose. Sooner her than me. I don't like these foreigners. Never know what they're going to get up to. Specially the gents. I think they're the worst of the lot.'

'Oh yes? Foreign, was he? French, or what?'

'No, not French. Not German either. What did you think he was, Annie?'

Annie shrugged.

'Search me. Just foreign. Funny name. Never heard it before. Vlad I think he said.'

'Vlad?' repeated Edie. 'What kind of a name is that?'

'Who knows? Anyway, you know what those foreign names are. They sound all glam, and that. Then you find that in the bloke's own country it's the same as Bert Smith would be, here.'

'That's right enough.'

Annie said thoughtfully, 'bit of a gent though really. Bought us a drink. I mean, all of us. Didn't have to do that. He only wanted one.'

Sandra laughed.

'Wanted Mollie, 'cause of her black hair. Kinky.'

'He never said that,' objected Annie. 'He said, the lady with the raven tresses. That's what he said.'

'Raven tresses, my ass,' snorted Edie. 'Oh, I get my raven tresses from Boots the Chemist. Where d'you get your golden tresses, Sandra?'

'Same place. Next shelf up.'

Annie ignored them.

'Said she reminded him of Lucy. She would be his Lucy. Must have been his missus, I s'pose.'

'Smile, girls,' whispered Sandra. 'Business.'

A group of middle-aged men had approached the table.

'Evening, girls. Mind if we join you?'

*   *   *

Sue Duncan stood sideways to the full-length mirror, smoothing unnecessarily at the flatness of her stomach. At the same time she checked critically at her rear, to be certain she wasn't deceiving herself by pulling herself in at the front, only to project at the back. But she need not have worried. She was flat and trim as a seventeen year old in top physical condition. Not bad for an old lady of twenty eight.

What time was it? Oh, good. Almost an hour before she had to keep her date. Sitting down at the dressing table she picked up a bottle of hand cream, and began to massage gently at the backs of her hands. She was feeling strangely discontented tonight. No reason for it, really. He seemed a nice enough man, and there was no doubt she would enjoy the theatre. This particular play was very difficult to book, and it was only because he was a visitor to London, and paying through the nose of course, that they were able to get in. Oh, the show would be all right. Supper, too. He seemed like the type who'd want to do everything properly. Sue hoped he would take her to supper. That way, she could be certain of help from her old ally, the wine-cellar. Not that she didn't usually enjoy what came afterwards, if the man knew what he was

79

doing, but there was always this nagging feeling, the consciousness of wrong-doing. And it would be considered wrong by most people, even in these enlightened times. A young married woman, off out partying while her husband was away for the night, because of his job. Stretched out on a bed in some plush hotel room, with a man she hardly knew. Well, what was she supposed to do? A perfectly healthy young woman, with normal appetites?

But what about Donald? they would ask. Such a nice man. Hard-working, sober, reliable. Always kept the garden tidy. That was all they saw. That was all anyone saw, outside of Sue herself. They didn't see him disappear upstairs, night after night, leaving her to her own devices. When they were first married, Donald Duncan was a normal young man. Rather serious, most of the time, but with a streak of fun in him, which would suddenly thrust itself forward at the most unexpected times. A hearty eater, and a vigorous man in the bedroom. A man who could please a woman, and Sue had responded to him gladly. But, after his South American trip, all that had changed. A stay of only a few days, in a fever-ridden swamp area, had induced some blood-wasting disease that had turned Donald into a walking skeleton for a while. Local tribesmen, reputed to be devil-worshippers, had saved his life by their own methods, but he returned to the civilised world a different man. Secretive, withdrawn. Alien, to the point of open hostility, until Sue became physically afraid to question him.

Then, finally, he had decided to move into the spare bedroom. From there, it was a short step to the point where he spent all his free time in the room. He kept the door locked for a time, but then, after a series of violent accusations that she was spying on him, he had secured the door with a padlock and chain.

On one occasion, when he was out of the house, she had carried a ladder to the rear, and climbed up to look in at his window. Everything was draped in black. Close to the window, there stood what seemed to be some kind of altar. At each side rested a tall silver candlestick, which Sue had never seen before, and between these, three silver dishes. Hung carefully behind the door was a black velvet cloak, with red satin lining. That must have cost him a month's pay. But for what? There was a row of books, stacked sideways to her, so that she could only identify one title. Vampire Lore, it was called. Strange. But no stranger than the hideous stuffed figure of a bat on the wing, suspended from the ceiling, its red eyes seeming to stare malevolently into her own. What could it all mean? What on earth was he doing in that evil room? For it was evil, she could feel it, even through the closed windows.

The sudden slamming of a car door had almost made her lose her balance. She descended as quickly as she could, amazed to find that her hands, indeed her whole body, shook with unaccustomed fear. Donald had said nothing, although he must have noticed the ladder lying on the rear lawn. The next time she ventured out into the garden, it was to discover that the window was now blacked out. It had remained that way ever since.

Her life was totally unreal. She worked all day as the chief receptionist for a busy doctors' practice, then went home to—nothing. Nothing at all. There were times when she felt she might go mad, with the boring frustration of it all, coupled with her increasing fear of the sinister stranger to whom she was married. An attractive, vital young woman, she received her fair share of overtures from roving males, and had even been tempted on a few occasions. But she had always refused, partly because of her married status, but more and more because of her terror of Donald.

Then, a few months ago, had come a dramatic change in her life. Donald had changed his job. A graduate chemist, he had been engaged on research for years, and the decision to change came as a total surprise. Sue had not dared to ask for details, and none had been forthcoming, but she no longer really cared. The job took him and his new boss away about one night each week, sometimes more. For Sue it was like someone opening the gateway to freedom. Donald's nights away became her ticket to a new life, and she took it with both hands. There was always the risk that someone would see her, one of these nights, but it was slight. And even if they did, who would identify the dark beauty in the dress circle as the dispirited housewife from the suburban detached? She had often imagined the conversation.

'Oh look, Edwin. Isn't that woman like Mrs. Duncan?'

'Hmph. In Mrs. Duncan's dreams, perhaps. Wouldn't mind bumping into that one in the supermarket.'

'God, you are vulgar at times.'

She smiled at her own thoughts, as she sat before the mirror. He was young, this one tonight. Young, and with big shoulders. Strong. Probably a games player, rugby, perhaps? Sue picked up a bottle of perfume, inspected the label, changed her mind and substituted another. Tipping a few drops onto her fingers, she began to massage gently at her breasts. You won't be fit enough for the first fifteen this weekend, my boy. I'll see to that.

Where was it Donald had said he was going? Somewhere near Manchester, that was it. A good, long journey from Shaftesbury Avenue.

*   *   *

Bill Wallington leaned on the news editor's

desk.

'What's all the panic? I've got an hour yet.'

'Leave your notes. I'll get somebody to type it up. You're going out. Here.'

Wallington took the buff envelope, looking at the printed slip.

'Manchester? Come on, now. I've done my turn in the bleeding sticks for this week.'

'Bleeding sticks, did you say? Must be a mind reader.'

The reporter frowned.

'All right, so I don't get it. Was there a prize?'

His boss rested shirt-sleeved elbows on the desk.

'Do you remember a story you did once? Long time ago. About some vampire at a Horror Ball?'

'Oh come on, be fair. I've been bollocked for that. It's over.'

'Wrong. It's not over. I'm telling you officially that said bollocking is withdrawn. Don't know what evil god looks after you Bill, but you were right. Everybody else was wrong. Feel better?'

The surprise on Wallington's face was genuine.

'Well,' he whistled. 'That's practically handsome, coming from you. But how do we know? New evidence, is there?'

'Better than that. New body. Woman. Same wounds. Marks on the neck, arrow through the left breast, and suspected poisoning on top of that.'

'Wow.' He wagged the envelope. 'And it's somewhere in Manchester. This bloke must have a bicycle. I'm on my way.'

'Someone'll meet you at the airport. Better take all your stuff from that Great Bravington case.'

At the door, Wallington turned.

'Worth a by-line, this.'

'We'll see.'

*   *   *

Doctor Mary Newman yawned, smoothed her hair and knocked at the door.

'Come in.'

Doctor MacIntyre was busy reading the night reports.

'Oh hallo, doctor,' he greeted. 'It's been a busy night, by the look of things. This coach business is bad.'

He leaned back in his chair, tapping at the reports.

'These are medical reports, not newspapers of course. What actually happened, do we know?'

'Oh yes,' she began.

'I'm so sorry doctor, I should have asked you to sit down. You look all in.'

'Thank you. As I was saying, the police have been in and out a good deal, so we have a fair

85

picture of the scene. The coach party had been out to Cambridge. Some big get-together of dancing schools. There was a ball, very formal, you can't imagine some of the clothes. Then there was a late supper, and it was about one in the morning when they started back. They were on the London side of Harlow, on the M11, when this sports car came straight at them. The coach driver was in the fast lane, and all he could do was swerve. The driver of the car must have realised the danger at the same time, and unfortunately he did the same thing. The crash was not quite head-on.'

'That's the man who's dead? Er, Ian Paulson.'

'Yes. As you see, his blood was full of alcohol. I forget the figures.'

'Never mind. The woman with him, Susan Duncan. It seems hard to credit, not one broken bone.'

'She was extraordinarily lucky. In that sense, at least. There's still the concussion, of course. No telling what the long-term effect of that might be.'

'Quite so. The rest of it is just a saga of cuts and bruises. Except for the driver of course. Tell me about the others first. Any reason why they shouldn't all go home today?'

'Not unless we get some delayed shock. They've been very lucky. The driver too, in a way. Nice clean break to his right femur. No, it's the girl I'm worried about.'

MacIntyre was interested.

'It could be because I've been reading rather a heavy psychology text-book in the evenings, but I seem to detect an interest above the medical?'

Mary Newman smiled tiredly.

'Guilty, I'm afraid. She intrigues me. For a start, she's married—'

'Ah—'

'—so why was she rushing up the M11 in the middle of the night, with a man who wasn't her husband? The police think they may have been making for the new club, the Green Parrot. It's somewhere near Harlow, apparently. Perhaps you've heard of it?'

'It seems to ring a bell vaguely. What makes the police think that?'

'The man was a member. They found a card in his wallet.'

'I see. Well doctor, when anyone can explain to me why people do the things they do, I shall be a model listener. I shouldn't make too much of it. She could be his sister, for all we know.'

The duty doctor shook her head.

'Doubtful. He's only been in the country for a few days. He's—or rather he was— Australian. There's more than that. The girl seems to be in mortal fear of her husband. His name is Donald, by the way, and the police can't get any answer from the house. According to neighbours, his job keeps him away from home, on occasion.'

'Mortal fear? Drastic choice of words.'

'Yes. But justified. She has odd moments of lucidity. Seems to think her husband is the devil himself.'

Doctor MacIntyre laughed.

'She's probably making the point that there will be the very devil to pay when her husband finds out what she's been up to. I shouldn't make too much of it, doctor. It's been a long night, and you're tired. I should get off to bed if I were you.'

At the door she turned.

'I did ask to be contacted if there's any change in her condition. You won't—'

'Tell them to leave you alone? No, all right, if you're that interested.'

'Thank you, doctor.'

Doctor MacIntyre read again through the notes on the crash victim. Then he scribbled a quick rider at the foot, and turned the file over.

It was marked in clear, square capitals.

Duncan, Susan, Mrs.

CHAPTER SEVEN

The shining black limousine slowed, then swung between wide iron gates into a sweeping gravel drive.

Superintendent Vine looked out at a squad of marching cadets, very correct and military-looking in the morning sunshine. The main building came into view, a one-time country house now leading a new life as the County Police Training College. As the car stopped outside the huge wooden front door, a uniformed sergeant materialised, and stood waiting for him to emerge.

'Superintendent Vine, sir? This way, if you please.'

Vine thanked the driver, tucked his briefcase under his arm, and followed the sergeant inside.

'Lovely spot you have here, sergeant.'

'Yes, sir. We're very lucky, really. It would cost millions nowadays to build a place this size, not to mention the grounds.'

They turned left into a carpeted corridor.

'In here superintendent, if you please.'

The sergeant stood, holding open a door. Vine nodded his thanks and went inside.

'Superintendent Vine, sir,' called the sergeant.

'Morning, superintendent.'

From behind a leather-topped desk, a tall rangy man, with a bristling white moustache and fierce eyebrows, rose to meet him.

'I'm Appleton, Deputy Chief Constable. You've made good time.'

They shook hands, and Vine inspected his new host with interest. 'Happy' Appleton was widely known in police circles as an efficient administrator, with sometimes a touch of unorthodox behaviour which didn't always endear him to the powers-that-be.

Seated beside him was a pale faced, youngish man with a dark, silky beard. He rose as Appleton turned to introduce him, and Vine found himself being inspected by eyes of an astonishing clarity and depth.

'Let me introduce Professor Abraham Cornfeld, who acts as special consultant on Eastern European history to the Associated Northern Universities.'

Vine looked at the pale faced young man, whose handshake was firm enough. Professor of what? Eastern European history? Funny sort of geezer to bring in to an investigation. The professor may have been conscious of the kind of thinking his presence had prompted, but stared back at him unblinkingly.

Appleton waited until the formalities were over.

'Sit down, superintendent. Like some coffee?'

'No thank you, sir. I managed to get some on the train.'

'Then we'll get right down to it. Oh, do smoke if you wish.'

'Thank you, sir.'

Vine drew thankfully on his cigarette, and waited for his superior to explain what this visit was about. All he'd been told was to report to Mr. Appleton, and take his Great Bravington murder file with him. Appleton flicked down a switch on a small intercom unit.

'Ready when you are, Charlie,' he announced.

Within seconds, a door at the side of the room opened, and another man came in. Not a chap to meet down an alley on a dark night, thought Cornfeld. A little over medium height, the new arrival exuded brute strength from every corner of his broad, heavily muscled frame.

'Chief Superintendent Charlie Grayce,' announced Appleton. 'This is Superintendent Vine from the Wessex force.'

The two men shook hands and nodded, appraising each other as they did so.

'Good journey?' grunted Grayce.

'Not bad. On time, anyway.'

'Well, that's what counts.'

Grayce looked around uncertainly.

'Pull up a chair, Charlie.'

Appleton settled back, pressing the tips of his fingers together, and waited. Grayce dragged a chair across, and sat down to form a square with the other three.

'All we've said so far, Charlie, is good morning,' explained the deputy chief. 'Now we can start. First of all, Mr. Vine, will you say what you've been told already?'

Vine shrugged.

'Nothing at all. I got a message before I left

home. Shove my papers on the Great Bravington murder into a briefcase, get up here fast, and report to you, sir. That's all I know.'

'Ah,' nodded Appleton. 'Good. Then we start with a nice clean sheet. Last night, a common prostitute was murdered, on our patch. Nothing unusual there, you may think. She wasn't the first, and she certainly won't be the last. Hardly something unusual enough to justify the Deputy Chief Constable sticking his nose in. Isn't that right, Charlie?'

Chief Superintendent Charlie Grayce grinned faintly, but was not to be drawn. Appleton continued.

'In case you're thinking that Deputy Chief Constables should keep their great noses out of routine police enquiries, let me assure you that Chief Superintendent Grayce has already put your point of view forward. Forcefully, and at length. True, Charlie?'

Grayce fiddled with a pencil.

'I seem to recall something of that sort, sir,' he admitted.

Vine suppressed a grin. A man did not need to be a super-detective to know that there had been a hell of a ding-dong between these two a few hours earlier. Professor Cornfeld's face betrayed nothing.

Appleton grinned.

'I should hope you do,' he reproved. 'I shall carry the bruises for weeks. However, Mr.

Vine,' and he was serious again, 'this is not a case of me wanting to play Sherlock Holmes. As soon as I heard the first reports of this case, I began to get a feeling. A feeling which grew stronger by the hour, and which has brought you to this meeting. And, of course, Professor Cornfeld. Especially the professor. I'll tell you more about that as we go on. First of all, I want you to hear the bare facts of the case. Charlie, are you ready to take over now?'

Grayce opened the brown file he'd brought with him, nodding.

'Right,' said Appleton briskly. 'I'm going to hand over now to Chief Superintendent Grayce, who will give you a résumé. I would ask you please to make a note of your questions, and we'll deal with them at the end. I think it's better if we don't interrupt the chief super until then. Ready when you are, Charlie.'

Grayce cleared his throat.

'Because of the informal nature of this meeting,' he began, 'I'm not going to present this case as though we were in a courtroom. What I mean is, I'm not going to quote the number of every P.C. who's been involved. And I'm not going to say anything about proceeding in a northerly direction.'

He paused to let them grin at the small joke.

'There is a drinking club in Temple Street, known as The Crypt. In that Division we remember it better as the Captain's Cabin, and

93

before that Miss Ella's Joint. Same premises, same general clientele. In other words, a clip joint. Two quid for a gin and tonic, and a chance to pick up one of the girls. It is a known haunt of prostitutes. One of these was last night's victim. Name was either Margaret MacBride or Mollie MacBride. She's been convicted under both those names, at different times in the past. There could even be other names that we don't yet know, because the woman came here from Glasgow, just over a year ago. The Glasgow police are looking into this for us at this moment. Mostly, she was known as Irish Mollie. Age thirty-four, medium height, no known scars, jet-black hair—'

Professor Cornfeld made a scribbled note.

'—important point—' interrupted Appleton.

'—and by all accounts, quite a good-looking woman. The early part of our information about last night relies heavily on the words of other known prostitutes, and we all know how much faith we can put in what they have to say. Nevertheless. It seems fairly clear that the woman MacBride was drinking in The Crypt until approximately nine-thirty. There were two other street-women with her. A man approached all three, and bought a round of drinks.'

'This man seems to have been on the tall side, but probably less than six feet. Dark hair, very pale face. Age hard to determine. One

94

woman says thirty, the other one forty-five. The bartender, who is known to take quite an interest in the male customers, in fact, in males generally—'

—Vine pursed his lips—

'—says he would have placed the man's age at less than forty. But I should tell you that the lighting in the place is appalling. It is kept that way so that some of the women can pass for fifteen years younger than they are. This man spoke to them in a foreign accent. They all give different versions of what they mean by foreign. He gave them a name, which one woman said was Brad. The other one didn't agree. She said it sounded like Brad, but it wasn't Brad. He told them he was a nobleman of his own country, but they're used to hearing all kinds of yarns in The Crypt. Eventually he settled on McBride, as being the one he would leave with. Then he said one thing, on which both women were agreed. He spoke of McBride as having raven-tresses, and that he would call her Lucy.'

Vine started, and looked at the professor, who was busy writing.

'These two then left the club together. McBride had a flat a few minutes' walk away. We have not yet found any evidence that they drove from the club, either in a private car or in a taxi. No witnesses have come forward who can throw any light on their movements after leaving the club. But eventually they arrived at the flat. Some time between one a.m. and one thirty, a prostitute named Edith Norton, sometimes Brown, went to the flat to find McBride. It seems that Norton and McBride had arranged to meet some men at midnight, and there had been trouble when McBride did not appear. Norton was in some distress, because these men had said someone was going to be cut about if they did not get the party they had arranged for. McBride did not answer the door, but Norton knew where to find the spare key. She went into the flat. McBride was lying on the floor, dead. Her blouse had been ripped off, and a wooden arrow had been plunged through her left breast, piercing the heart. There was some blood on her throat, which was later identified as a bite. Our medical examiner produced further facts, which of course the woman Norton could not be expected to know.'

Grayce paused for a moment, sifted through the papers before him, and produced a single buff sheet.

'McBride did not die from the arrow thrust, but from some quick-acting poison. This poison, infiltrated the blood stream from a very small scratch on her arm. It is the doctor's opinion that with the smallness of the wound, it probably felt nothing more than a pinprick at the time. When the arrow entered the body, the woman was either dead already, or at the very least in the final stages of the deepest coma. That's our first point. Second point is that owing to the particularly fast action of this poison, blood coagulation is accelerated, enabling the police surgeon to fix the time of death with some precision. The time he has given us is between midnight and twelve-thirty. Third and last point. The murderer had made some unsuccessful attempt at intercourse with the dead woman.' The chief superintendent looked around at the assembled faces, and his voice was grave. 'This attempt was made after the woman was dead.'

He stopped speaking then, and the room was quiet for a few moments. The Deputy Chief Constable coughed slightly.

'Is that the end, chief super?'

'That's all for the immediate purposes of this meeting sir, thank you. I have the photographs, of course, and other details such as measurements and so forth which can be made available, if required.'

'Right. Well thank you for that very helpful rundown, and I think we can take questions now. Yes, Professor.'

Vine waited to hear what the silk-bearded professor was going to say. To his surprise, the voice was rich and deep, and could have belonged to a Shakespearean actor.

'In your excellent summary Mr. Grayce, you mentioned that this man bought the ladies a drink. Do you have a note of whether he drank with them, and if so, what he had?'

97

Grayce winced slightly at the word 'ladies', but referred back to his notes.

'No, I haven't a note about that, Professor. I imagine he must have done. Can't see a man buying drinks for three women, at those prices, and not having one himself.'

'Quite. But you have no evidence of it?'

'No.'

'Thank you. That was my only point.'

Appleton caught Vine's eye.

'Superintendent Vine.'

'Thank you, sir. More of a comment than a question. Mr. Grayce said that the victim had jet-black hair, and you said that was important.'

'I did.'

'Our victim's hair was black, also. But it was the business of the name which struck me. The man said he would call McBride Lucy, although her name was Mollie. With our case, we had one witness who was adamant he heard the name Lucy being used. Not once, but at least twice. Now, I must admit I discounted what he said at the time. You see, the name of our victim was Elizabeth. That seemed a natural mistake, for someone to hear the name Lizzy or Liz, and to think they'd heard Lucy. After what Mr. Grayce has told us, I'm not so sure.'

He was surprised to find the professor's eyes upon him, and a head nodding with approval.

'Thank you, Mr. Vine. Any more questions?'

There were a number, but Vine didn't want to voice them at this moment. His mind was harking back to the details of Elizabeth Warren's murder, and the number of points bearing a striking similarity to the case now being investigated by Chief Superintendent Grayce. No, dammit, it was no use thinking in terms of similarities. There could be no question about it. They were both dealing with the same man. What he really wanted was to confer with Grayce alone, but he could hardly start talking to the man as though no one else was present.

Appleton said,

'All done, superintendent? Professor? Right, well thank you for those points. You'll have every opportunity to come in again, never fear. At this stage, and before I ask Professor Cornfeld to speak to you, I'm going to take the floor myself for a few minutes. As I said before, I've taken an unusual step in calling this meeting, and I hope by the time I've finished explaining, you will agree that I was justified. For the benefit of Professor Cornfeld and Mr. Grayce, who won't have had the opportunity to brief themselves about the Great Bravington murder a few days ago, I shall start by giving a brief summary of that case. Superintendent Vine, I hope you'll correct me if I leave anything out.'

This brought a smile from Charlie Grayce, but Appleton shook his head.

'Oh, I'm not just being polite when I say that. It's absolutely vital that we all know all the facts. So I rely on you Superintendent to jump in if I'm going adrift.'

Vine nodded his understanding.

The Deputy Chief Constable then outlined the known facts about the Great Bravington murder. Vine listened intently, waiting for an omission or a mis-statement, but it was evident the chairman of the meeting had taken the closest possible interest in the progress of the case. In less than ten minutes he had set out all the major known points, and the visitor was compelled to admire the extent of the man's grasp. He had had no access to statements made by witnesses, naturally, and it could not be claimed that his knowledge was as deep as that of the man from Wessex. Nevertheless, it was a masterly exhibition.

'That's the situation as I have understood it, from outside,' he concluded. 'Would you wish to add anything, Mr. Vine?'

Vine wagged his head from side to side.

'There are odd details, little tidbits that we know from people we interrogated, sir, but they don't alter anything of what you have said. Or even add much to it.'

Appleton smiled.

'Thank you. Doubtless, if you think they are important, as we proceed, you will refer to

100

them. Very well, then. In case you are wondering why I should have taken such a close interest in a matter being dealt with by another force, I will tell you. It was the way the story was dealt with by the Daily Chronicle. I can see by your faces that some of you read it. What interested me was that this particular newspaper should go off at such a tangent from all the rest. When you put the story next to the treatments given by the other national dailies, you would scarcely know it was the same case. I was fascinated that such an important paper could so mislead itself, never mind the readers. And I studied that story, trying to understand how anyone could have linked up those tiny pointers to make such a sweeping allegation. From there, it was only a short jump to a fantasy world. There's no end to that stuff once you get started on it. It so happened that I was having lunch with Abe Cornfeld, and I knew he was something of an expert. We spent half an hour chatting about it. Just social chit-chat, really. I was surprised that he didn't find it all that far-fetched.'

The two police officers looked at each other. Abraham Cornfeld had suddenly become Abe, and a personal friend of the deputy chief's. It was a useful pointer as to how to address him when the time came.

'Anyway,' Appleton went on, 'as I say it was just a social occasion, and I put it from my mind. Until today. As soon as Charlie Grayce

101

told me about the McBride murder, all my earlier thoughts came back with a rush. Instead of asking him to keep me posted, which I would normally do, I jumped in with both feet. I have a feeling about this, gentlemen. Not just a casual feeling either. One that was strong enough to prompt me to ask the Chief Constable of Wessex if Mr. Vine could attend this meeting. Strong enough for me to ask Professor Cornfeld if he could join us. He had to cut into a very busy schedule to be here, and I'm most grateful to him. In fact, with time so important to all of us, I've arranged an al fresco lunch in the office. Hope you don't mind.'

Almost as though someone on the outside was clairvoyant, the door opened, and there was a rattling of trolleys.

'Ah, here come our refreshments. This is a suitable time to break off. I'm not going to suggest we talk as we eat. Don't want butter all over the coroner's reports. Just help yourselves, gentlemen, and let's have twenty minutes off.'

Two young women P.C.s were setting out plates on a table by the wall. The meeting broke off.

CHAPTER EIGHT

'I say, those smell good.' Vine pointed to a large centre plate. 'What are they?'

'Chicken vol-au-vents,' replied one of the girls. 'Janet used to be a cook before she joined the force.'

'Good for Janet. Can I take two?'

'I don't see why not, sir. The chief super's already got three.'

Vine helped himself, picked up his beer and went to join Charlie Grayce.

'Your boss is going overboard a bit on this lot isn't he?' queried Vine.

Grayce nodded.

'Hope he knows what he's doing. There'll be a bleeding uproar if he's got this wrong. Bringing you up here, and everything.'

Vine bit into a ham sandwich, neatly caught an escaping slice of tomato with his other hand, and popped it into his mouth.

'Does he do this sort of thing?' he asked. 'I mean, is he a bit erratic?'

'Not a bit. Very sound copper. Very cautious, as a rule. Some people even think he's a bit of a stick-in-the-mud. This is right out of character. Well, I did warn him.'

Vine chuckled.

'Way he spoke, it sounded as though you had a proper old barney.'

'Not really. But I did have to let him know what I thought.'

The superintendent nodded agreement.

'Of course you did. You didn't think much of his theory, then? About us both chasing the same bloke?'

'Oh, I wouldn't go that far. It's not impossible, I suppose. But he's done it all in such a rush. Dammit, I haven't even completed my preliminary enquiries yet, never mind started a proper investigation. Still, he's done it, and that's that.'

He was about to say more, but checked himself when he noticed the professor approaching.

'Excuse me, I'll just get some more of this grub.'

'Superintendent Vine.'

A deep voice in his ear brought him round to face Professor Cornfeld.

'Hallo, Professor.'

'I know I must be very careful not to upset your police protocol. Is it in order for me to talk to you, without your hosts being present?'

Vine grinned.

'Well, I'm allowed to talk, yes. Might have to be a bit careful what I say, that's all.'

The professor nodded. How old would he be, the superintendent wondered. He looked very young for a professor. Probably no more than thirty.

'The aspect of the case which intrigues me

more than any other is the intervention of the man Nosferatu.'

The policeman shivered.

'Ugh. Creepy character, that. You know, when you've been a copper a few years, there aren't many types of people you haven't met. But I've never come across anybody remotely like him before. Hope I never do again. He hasn't turned up on this case, has he?'

'Not to my knowledge. Not so far, that is. It will not surprise me if he does put in an appearance.'

'Well, I hope I've gone home before he does.'

He said it so fervently that the professor smiled.

'He must have made quite an impression on you. You seemed to shiver just now.'

'Just thinking about him gives me the shivers. And everybody else who saw him, too. Can't describe it, really. He seems to carry an air of death about him. Sound like an old lady, don't I?'

Cornfeld shook his head.

'No. Mr Vine, you do not. I would think you have probably described him very well. Ah, we seem to be resuming.'

The others had begun to sit down again. Appleton was already in position, and looking at his watch. Vine settled back in his seat.

The chairman had started speaking.

'Let's get back to it, gentlemen. By the way,

smoke if you wish. Don't like it at meetings, as a rule, but since we didn't have a proper lunch break, it won't hurt for once.'

So saying, he produced an evil-looking black briar, and began to stuff it with shag. The two policemen lit cigarettes.

'Just to recap, then, I was saying that I have very strong views about the connection between the McBride murder here last night, and the Great Bravington case. I'm going to hand over now to Professor Cornfeld, but before I do, let me remind you of his special subject, which is Eastern European history. He has acted as adviser to the British Museum on more than one occasion, and made a great number of television appearances on historical matters. The professor is one of the two or possibly three leading experts in the country, and I want you to pay particular attention to what he has to tell us. If you please, Professor.'

Cornfeld looked around the table, stroking his beard and smiling gently.

'Thank you, Mr. Appleton,' he began. 'Gentlemen, I shall try to keep my story as brief as possible. I am anxious to avoid it's taking on the semblance of a lecture. For one thing, this is not a classroom. For another, we all know what happens if people attend lectures after lunch. They fall asleep. That I do not want. As Mr. Appleton has told you, my special study is the history of Eastern Europe, and you may well be wondering what connection that can possibly have with two separate murder cases in the United Kingdom. I shall hope to convince you that the connection exists.'

There was a bulging briefcase down by the side of his chair. Leaning down, he clicked it open.

'But first, let us talk of fiction. A small masterpiece of fiction, in my view.'

He brought out a slim volume and placed it on the table.

'Many of you will have read this, at some time in your lives. It was written in 1897, and has been in print ever since. The author was a man named Bram Stoker. The title of the book is "Dracula".'

Vine swallowed, and shifted in his seat.

'Because this book was, and is, so successful, people have come to think of the character of Dracula as a fiction. Indeed, as portrayed by the author, this is largely true. But that is by no means all there is to it. The fact,' and he tapped on the table to be certain of attention, 'the fact is that there was an actual historical person by that name. A prince, not a count as described. A bloodthirsty, barbarous man who caused the death quite certainly of hundreds, and even possibly thousands of innocent people.'

He reached down into his bag again and pulled out a folded linen map which he proceeded to open flat on the table. Everyone leaned forward.

'This is Eastern Europe as it was four hundred years ago. In today's terms it was bounded on the west by Yugoslavia, and on the east by the Black Sea and Turkey. To the north, going from left to right, the countries we now know as Germany, Poland, Soviet Russia.' He described a rough circle in the centre of the map. 'This hinterland is what we know as Hungary, Roumania and Bulgaria. In those days there was a Hungary and a Bulgaria, but there were other states, too. Moldavia, for one. And, more particularly to our purpose, Wallachia. Here. The river that you see is the Danube.'

The professor made a point of identifying the river, because it would be a familiar name to his audience, and thus add authenticity to what was to follow.

'Wallachia was a primitive feudal state governed by a succession of people, none of them for very many years at a time. One of these warrior princes was a man named Vlad Dracul—no, this is not our man. Not yet. Dracul was bad enough in his own way, as the very name tells us. Dracul is the word for dragon or devil. But he had a son, who ruled from time to time after him. His name was also Vlad, and he became known as Vlad Tepes, which means Vlad the Impaler. Ah, I see you are paying close attention, Superintendent Vine.'

'Indeed I am, Professor. Please don't let me interrupt.'

'As the son of Dracul, this man was also called Dracula. So there is your historical reality. As to his own descriptive title, The Impaler, he earned this by his devilish habit of skewering people on wooden stakes. I need not dwell on the details, I think. Everyone suffered, if they crossed his path. Men, women, children. The man was capable of the most unspeakable cruelties. Now, enough history.'

The faces around him showed clear disappointment.

'Those, then, are just a few of the bare facts. Now, this region of which we have been speaking is a land of superstitious peasants. Their minds are unusually attuned to things of darkness. I am not by any means an expert on myths and legends, and I make this quite clear. However, I am able to say with authority that the folklore of this entire region is concerned, to a very high degree, with vampires, werewolves, and other man-beast manifestations. There are even protective measures to be taken against such creatures. Garlic, poppy seeds, wild rose thorns are all prescribed in the legends, as also is the cross. Ideally, the cross should be made from the wood of the wild rose. These are protective only. The only actual destruction of a vampire is much more difficult, and often quite unspeakable. One of the least savage of the prescriptions requires the severing of the head, and its destruction by fire. The most popular, and this is what our Mr. Stoker included in his fine story, is to drive a wooden stake through the body. This stake, again, should be made from the wood of the wild rose, or from an ash tree. It is, of course, common to many of these fairy tales, for that is what they are, that blood is sucked from the neck of a victim.'

Cornfeld stopped speaking, and left the room silent while he lit a cigarette. Next to him, Grayce wrinkled his nose. Turkish?

'Very briefly then, to sum up. There are two parts to my little address. The factual, sketchy though it necessarily is. The mythical, which is far more abundant in detail and quantity, and entirely unreliable. To understand the reasoning which we now present to you, it is essential that these two, the true and the false, be kept in separate compartments.'

He looked along the table at Appleton, who nodded.

'Thank you, Professor. I'm quite sure none of the class fell asleep. It was all much too interesting. From now on, we will take it in turns, if that is agreeable.'

The professor inclined his head, and Appleton continued.

'Leaving to one side the circumstances of our two murders for the moment, let us look at the similarities. One, both victims were poisoned, and in the same manner, by a scratch on the arm. Two, there were bite marks on the neck. Three, there was an arrow driven forcibly through the heart. Four, both murders were committed under cover of darkness. Five, both victims had black hair. Six, both were addressed by the murderer as Lucy. Professor.'

'Yes. Then there was the name. In the case of McBride, the witnesses could not agree that the man, the foreign man, called himself Brad. I think they could not agree, because they did not hear correctly. I think the murderer described himself as Vlad. Superintendent Vine, be so good as to help us with your case. This intriguing man you spoke with, Nosferatu. Did he not volunteer his suggestion about the murderer's self-deception as to his identity?'

Vine nodded, clearing his throat.

'Yes, he did. To use Nosferatu's own words, he said the murderer thought himself that which he was not. He thought he was Vlad Tepes.'

This brought some murmuring.

'Thank you,' acknowledged Cornfeld. 'It was this statement which prompted me to take a special interest. Clearly this Nosferatu, whether he be madman or imposter, or whatever, is an expert. He knows the subject. He could distinguish between the fact and the myth, as I can. What he was telling us, in his

111

own way, was that the murderer is not such an expert. He confuses the two. The man probably has a very disturbed mind, disturbed enough even to deceive himself that he is some kind of reincarnation of Dracula. But he does not have the kind of knowledge necessary to make such a deception accurate.'

Grayce wagged his head uncertainly.

'I'm sorry, professor, and I wasn't asleep, really, but I don't see how you can say that. Not on the strength of what we've been told so far. Unless I'm missing something?'

The professor listened very carefully.

'Very well, and I'm glad you have asked. Indeed, I hope any of you will ask questions, as you feel the need. You are asking how the murderer is failing in his impersonation. First, there is the poison. This has no place in any of the known facts, neither does it feature in the legends. Then there is the arrow itself. It should not be beyond the wit of an average intelligent man to fashion a pointed piece of wood. Of the proper wood. These arrows are both made of pine. Finally, the dark-haired girl named Lucy. That, gentlemen, is the clincher, as they say. There is no Lucy, either in history or legend. The only place where there is any reference to a girl by that name,' and he picked up the bound novel, 'is in Bram Stoker's novel. Our murderer is no phantom. No devil-worshipper, worthy of the name. He is our old friend, the homicidal maniac, with

112

Dracula-like hallucinations.'

He paused to let these words sink in. Those present looked at each other uneasily, or stared glumly at the table. The professor had just presented them with every policeman's nightmare. The man who kills on impulse, without motive, without rhyme or reason. The most unpredictable, and therefore elusive, of all offenders.

Charlie Grayce chimed in.

'Could I say a word, chairman?'

'Of course, Charlie.'

'I've been very impressed with what the professor has had to say. Very impressed indeed. I hope he won't be offended if I add a rider to that. I know from experience that it's rather easy to let yourself be carried along when you're listening to an expert. It's obvious that's what the professor is. A real expert. So, in the first place, I wouldn't like to rush into any conclusions immediately after hearing him. I'd like to think about it. If we're not careful, we could commit ourselves here today, and live to regret it when we've had a chance to think a bit more deeply. That's my first point.' He looked around. 'My second point is, even if we agree with what we've been told, the newspapers won't play it down. It's too good an angle, far too good, for them to ignore. We all saw what a splash the Chronicle made with the Great Bravington job. That wasn't much more than inspired guesswork, and it sent

113

shivers down a few spines. This time they'll all be at it. We're going to have a Dracula scare on our hands, whether we like it or not. That's all I wanted to say, sir.'

He could tell by Vine's face that he agreed. He was surprised to see that his chief was nodding vigorously.

'Glad you said that, Charlie. You're reading my mind again. For the benefit of those who don't know me, let me say that I'm not some Flash Harry who got this job because his mother runs the Hunt Ball. I'm a hard-nosed working copper, who came from the same background as anybody here. I'm not given to flights of fancy. Charlie has made two points. First of all, he wants a chance to think. I agree. It's my intention that the professor and I withdraw in a few minutes, so that you can discuss this freely. We'll be available to return when you're ready. But we must reach our decision as to how we're going to proceed, and we must do it today. Yes, Mr. Vine?'

Vine had wagged a pencil for attention.

'With respect, sir, I don't think I can commit my superiors without going back to them. I can give my opinion, naturally, and I will, but I haven't the authority to speak for my Chief Constable.'

'I have already explained the situation to him,' Appleton replied. 'He has indicated to me that he will be quite prepared to follow your advice, after this meeting. If you will telephone him, it can be cleared up on the spot.'

'I see. Thank you.'

'Now. As to Charlie's second point, the one about the gentlemen of the press. He is absolutely right once again. They are going to have a field day with this job, whether we like it or not. It is one more reason why we must all speak with one mind. What we can't have is a lot of chat about police uncertainty, top brass disagreements, rubbish like that. We make our decision, and by God we stand by it. I don't know whether any of you looked in the press room as you came in. I certainly didn't, but I had it monitored. They're all there, even the Sundays. Among them, large as life, is the chap who wrote the original Chronicle story, Bill Wallington. So, once we leave this room, we'll be on every front page in the country. Professor, do you want to say anything before we leave?'

'Thank you, no.'

'Very well. Charlie Grayce will know where to find us. Please be quite open with each other about every aspect. There'll be no chance for a rethink.'

CHAPTER NINE

After the door closed, there was silence in the room for a few moments. Then Chief Superintendent Grayce expelled breath in a low whistling sound.

'Well, what do you make of this lot?' he asked. 'Oh, call me Charlie, by the way. It's Alec, isn't it?'

'Thank you, yes it is. As to this little lot, well, I'm a bit shaken to tell you the truth.'

Vine was relieved at the friendly tone adopted by Charlie Grayce. His own position was precarious enough, and other people might well have resented his presence, and reacted accordingly. Evidently the home team were prepared to be receptive.

'Shaken? How do you mean?'

Alec Vine shrugged.

'I'm only a copper. Never been anything else. I never have enjoyed a case yet where the trick cyclists get involved. I know this bloke Cornfeld isn't one of those, but he still worries me, with his vampires and his legends. Personally, I prefer fingerprints to tooth marks.'

Grayce had been listening impassively. Now, a small grin appeared in one corner of his mouth.

'Know what you mean,' he grunted. 'Still,

116

have to admit the bloke knows his stuff. My reservation is whether his knowledge has any relevance to my case. Sorry, our case.'

It was the ultimate concession. Vine made up his mind, and held out a brown folder.

'This is our file on the Great Bravington job. It's all in there. Mind you, when I say "all", it doesn't amount to much. And here,' he extended an exercise book, 'are my own notes.'

Grayce took them, nodding. He recognised the importance of the gesture. To be handed the official file from another force was unusual in itself, but no more than his due, in the circumstances. To be made privy to the private thoughts of the man from Wessex was another matter entirely. It was the last word in cooperation, the personal contact.

'Appreciate that,' he muttered. 'Only thing is, I can't reciprocate. Haven't had a chance to do any thinking yet. All I've got is our official stuff, and even that is by no means complete. You're welcome to that, naturally.'

His folder was a different colour, and even slimmer than Vine's.

'I quite understand that, Charlie. What do you say we spend a few minutes reading these, before we try to compare notes?'

'I say yes.'

They settled down to the papers. Vine had a slight advantage, because there was so much less to read. This meant he was able to give more time to points of detail, and could let his mind roam more freely. He was aware too of his other advantage, which was his familiarity in depth with every aspect of the Great Bravington case. Chief Superintendent Grayce had not yet had time to study everything so completely.

What he did not then know was Grayce's enormous capacity for absorbing information at a glance. The man soaked up facts like a sponge, and his ability to recall the most abstruse scraps of information was legendary among his subordinates. After ten minutes, he had a very complete picture of the first murder. He raised his head, to find Vine ready to talk.

'H'm,' he uttered, 'very comprehensive. Makes you think, doesn't it?'

'It does,' agreed the Wessex man. 'Do you want to go first?'

'No, I don't think so. You've been at it longer than me. What do you make of it?'

Vine lit a cigarette, and began.

'It strikes me we're going to have to tackle this on two levels. First, there's the police work. I think there's enough similarity here for us to assume that we need cooperation between the two forces. Full exchange of all information, naturally. Plus, if you're agreeable, any feelings we get in the matter. You and me, that is.'

'I agree with that,' Grayce inclined his head portentously. 'What's your other level?'

'Your governor,' was the frank reply. 'Whether I agree with him or not, he's still a deputy chief constable. We ought to be prepared to go along with him, within reason. But, at the same time, I don't fancy committing myself to anything too fancy. I'd like to suggest that whatever we do in regard to his big theory, it shouldn't be something we couldn't withdraw from later, if it's going to make us all look like chumps.'

'Ha.'

Grayce stood up, walked a couple of quick paces away, turned, came back, and sat down just as abruptly.

'Agreed,' he announced. 'With reservations. You don't know Mister Happy Bleeding Appleton like I do. He's not one of these people you can agree with to his face, then go outside and do the opposite. If he thinks we're just being polite to humour him, he'll chop our heads off. Make no mistake about that. In fact, he'll chop off anything else that presents itself, at the same time. You say you don't want to look like a chump. Well, I'd sooner have that than a squeaky voice, if you see what I mean.'

Vine winced.

'He can be that rough, can he?'

'Rougher,' he was assured. 'Anyway, there's no immediate problem in that direction. We've got plenty of copper's work to do before we start issuing identikit pictures with fangs. Let's get started on that.'

It was evident that Grayce was not going to be rushed into any confrontation with his deputy chief, and in any case he was perfectly right. They had plenty to keep them busy for the time being. Vine smiled his agreement.

'Right, then. Let's talk about our killer. I think we know a great deal about him now. That is, if we are going to assume we both want the same man?'

'We'll have to, for now. Suppose you go through all this information we now have? All I've got so far is a description from a couple of half-sloshed whores.'

There was a hint of suspicion in his tone, and Vine realised he would have to tread carefully. He had, after all, the benefit of several days hard thinking behind him, as opposed to Grayce's few hours of high-speed fact-gathering. It wouldn't do for him to go charging ahead too quickly, creating an impression of the bright boy from outside, called in because the local fuzz couldn't cope.

'I've spent a lot of time trying to get a picture of this man. Trying to understand him, classify him. And, because the murder was on my patch, I've given a lot of attention to local detail, local people. Well, now I scrap all that, for a start.'

'Not necessarily,' objected Grayce. 'It could still be someone from your district who did this little job up here.'

'Completely agreed,' nodded Vine. 'And if it

120

was, we'll have him in a cage inside twenty four hours. There can't be more than a handful of people from one small area who would have any reason to be in Manchester at a particular time. My people will suss them out in record time, believe me. And if one of them fits, we've got him.'

He paused, to give Grayce an opportunity to come back, but the chief super merely inclined his head.

'That's the first thing, then. If he is one of mine, we'll have him, and quickly. But if we discount that for a moment, let's consider what we know about him. This poison, for example, is tremendously important. Your lab people haven't had time for analysis yet, but if we assume the same poison was used both times, then the lab report on my file will do for both. Now, as we both know, plenty of people have access to poisons of one kind and another, but this stuff is not a routine drug, nor an industrial usage type. It is an extremely virulent haemotoxin.'

Grayce squinted across at him.

'You mean I couldn't just pop into the chemist's and buy some?'

'Right. Nor could you get it from your garden shop. And, if you happened to work in some chemical plant, you still couldn't get it.'

'Ah.'

Grayce hunched himself forward, all attention.

'You mean I would have to be a doctor, or a chemist perhaps, before they'd let me have it?'

'Not even quite that, I'm afraid, although you're right about the doctor/chemist angle. You see, the stuff doesn't really exist, not in any ready form. It has no known application, either medical or industrial. It has to be made up specially. That means knowledge of what to do, and access to the materials. Still, as you say, a doctor or a chemist would have to do it.'

'We're talking about tens of thousands of people,' Grayce pointed out.

'No. We're talking about a lot less than that. Think of your doctors. They're in practice, or in hospitals, or in some form of Government service. Think of your chemists. They're in their own shops, or some industrial plant, some research project. They're working chaps, all of 'em. Can't just say to people "shan't be here tonight. Have to pop off and butcher a dark-haired girl. Back tomorrow".'

'I'm beginning to like this. Our man is on the move, of course. Out of tens of thousands of qualified people, we're down suddenly to what? A few hundred?'

'At the most, I would say. If the reasoning is right, then we have some old-fashioned police work to do. Notices, enquiries, the lot. With such a narrow field, I would guess we'll be down to a couple of dozen prospects inside a week. Well, Charlie, what do you think of it?'

Grayce banged a great palm against his

122

knee.

'I like it. I definitely like it. This is the stuff to give the coppers. Not your werewolves, but a nice bent doctor.'

'If we're right,' interjected Vine cautiously.

But Grayce was not to be put off now. Here was something a man could get his teeth into. Something positive, a good solid enquiry.

'We'd be mugs not to pursue this,' he said decisively, 'We'll go on looking at everything else, naturally, but I'm going to get a bet down on this Doctor X.'

Alec Vince held back on some other points he would have liked to make. It was clear that Charlie Grayce had made up his mind, for the moment at least. The atmosphere was harmonious, the cooperation one hundred per cent. It would have been foolish to jar their relationship by interposing some of his more remote thinking on the case. And, of course, from a purely practical point of view they had reached a very fruitful conclusion. Here was an enquiry which was both logical and satisfying. He smiled.

'Right. Now, what about your governor? And how are we going to muzzle the press?'

Grayce's brown eyes darkened momentarily.

'Yes,' he agreed glumly. 'They won't be put off too easily. Too good a story, this is. Damned if I know what to tell 'em. You got any ideas, Alec?'

Vine shook his head.

'Nothing of any value, I'm afraid. I'm a police officer, not a public relations geezer.'

'Right,' was the heartfelt rejoinder. 'Anyway, there's no reason why we should let it get us down. Let him deal with it, Appleton, I mean, he's the big public speaker. The press is part of his job. I'll go and get him, if you're ready?'

'Ready as I will be.'

Alone in the room, Vine walked over to the window and stared out at the grounds. He couldn't erase from his mind the face of Professor Cornfeld, and the sound of that knowing, persuasive voice. Alone among the people in this place, Vine had faced the chilling man/thing called Nosferatu. A certain amount of imagination was permitted in a police officer's make up, and indeed, as he climbed higher, it became a special part of his contribution. But within limits. Imaginative conjuring with material things, facts, dates, evidence, could often produce results. But the ground-rules were clear, the limits defined, and they did not permit flights of fancy. Did not permit the icy darkness in his stomach whenever he harked back to that confrontation at the Great Bravington Country Club. Inspector Cornwell had felt it, much as he had, but neither would have admitted it to the other. Too unpolicemanlike. And, he admitted privately, it might not even sound very manly. After all, what was there to tell anyone? That he'd encountered a rather weird sort of man at three o'clock in the morning, on a murder investigation? People would wonder whether he'd been overdoing it lately. Whether a few days fishing might not be the answer.

But the professor was different, Vine could sense it. He wouldn't pack him off, with advice to take more water with it. The professor would understand. The difficulty was that Vine was miles off his patch, and any attempt on his part to speak to the man privately would be a grave breach of etiquette.

Behind him, the door opened, and he turned to see the Deputy Chief Constable coming towards him, talking animatedly to Grayce. They both looked cheerful enough.

'Must say,' boomed Appleton, 'this sounds pretty good, Alec. You don't mind the "Alec"?'

'Of course not, sir. You think we might be onto something then?'

Appleton beamed.

'I'm sure of it. Put my shirt on it. Anway, it confirms one of my staple theories.'

Vine was puzzled. He wasn't familiar with the Deputy Chief's approach, but he could see a knowing grin on Charlie's face.

'Which one's that, sir?' he ventured.

'Put two coppers in a room, close the door, and leave to brew. When you open the door, they will have come up with something called a line of enquiry. Never fails, I assure you.'

The man was positively bouncing with good humour, and his smile was infectious.

'Well sir, if you're satisfied, it sounds as if we've all got plenty to keep us busy.'

'Right. Absolutely right. Now, as to the press angle—' Appleton looked at each in turn—'got to be careful. Circumspect. And that's putting it mildly. Any mention, even any hint of a doctor being involved in this, and there'll be bloody uproar. I shouldn't need to remind you of that, but I'm saying it anyway, so that there's no possibility of any misunderstanding. Bloody uproar, I do assure you. Every medical body in the country will be shouting for our blood, especially mine. Lawsuits will be as thick on the ground as snow in winter. Some of them from outfits we didn't even know existed. National Association for the Prevention of Footrot, I shouldn't wonder. But I'm sure you both know what I mean.'

'Absolutely, sir,' nodded Vine. 'What about taking the Press into our confidence? Do you think that might work?'

Appleton made a face.

'Dicey. Very dicey. Depends on how it's put across, really. If I can persuade them it's in the best interests of the public etc. Then they'll probably cooperate. They won't stand for me suppressing news, of course. That's understood. But if the atmosphere is right, I can probably get them to tone it down.'

'But you said it might be dicey,' Vine reminded him.

A shrug of the shoulders.

'Yes. Because I'm speaking of the big boys, the ones with the national coverage. I can talk to them, done it before. As I say, we can probably hammer out some kind of understanding. Unfortunately, they're not the only ones involved. Every little tick with some kind of right to a Press card is waiting to hear what we have to say. Wouldn't like to guarantee we could trust 'em all, agreement or not. Always some little snurge who's waiting for his big break, his chance to get his name on the breakfast tables.'

Charlie Grayce made a clucking sound.

'Well sir, what's the alternative?'

Appleton shrugged again.

'Don't think there is one. There's too much known already about our little case here, and too many people have lined it up with Alec's job. If I could splash about with my whitewash brush, I'd do it. But it's too late. No, gentlemen. Dicey it may be, but there's no way round it. I'm just going to have to ask them to play it very softly. All we can do is to hope they'll agree, and work our bleeding heads to catch this maniac, before one of them gets impatient and blows the gaff. Alec—'

'Sir?'

'—don't want 'em getting their teeth into you. Oh, sorry, no joke intended. I think the best place for you is gone. Any real need for you and Charlie to talk any more, at the moment?'

Vine and Grayce looked at each other.

'Well no, sir, I suppose not, really. I would have liked a bit more time, and I expect Charlie would too.'

Grayce agreed.

'Yes, we could have done with a bit more polishing. Still, we've both got telephones, and there's nothing major at the moment, I don't think. If it's important to get you away, I couldn't really justify asking you to stay.'

'That's it, then,' decided Appleton. 'I'll have transport waiting for you in five minutes. I'm afraid your departure won't be quite as posh as your arrival, Alec, but you can see the sense of it. We'll smuggle you out in a baker's van. Kitchen entrance.'

He stuck out his hand.

'Tell your gaffer I'm very grateful for the cooperation, won't you? And my personal thanks to you, for the trouble you've taken.'

'Pleasure sir. Let's hope we have him soon.'

The Deputy Chief swung round to Grayce.

'See him off please, Charlie. I'll go and have a quiet think before I see the gentlemen of the press.'

He was gone, and the two officers exchanged a grin. 'Done much riding in bakers' vans, have you?'

'Not a lot. but I think I'll prefer it to what he'll be doing in a few minutes' time.'

'Gawd, yes. No comparison. Well, we've

128

only got five minutes. Better get these papers sorted out.'

They tidied up their files, and a few minutes later, Grayce led Vine out through the kitchens. There were rich baking and roasting smells in the air. Vine's stomach gurgled unhappily.

'Smells good,' he muttered.

'It is good,' Grayce assured him. 'Feed 'em like fighting cocks out here. Still, they've got twenty years of meat pies and sandwiches after they pass out.'

'True.'

At the rear entrance, a white-painted van waited. The plain inscription on the side read 'Harry Trumpton, Family Baker'. Vine paused.

'Just a minute. Do I have to sit on the floor all the way back to the station?'

Grayce smiled knowingly.

'No need. There's bench seats both sides. Also riot shields, helmets and batons. Very aggressive sort of baker, our Harry.'

'Ah.'

The rear door stood open. The two men shook hands.

'Good luck at this end,' said Vine.

'And at yours,' grunted Charlie. 'Race you to the bastard, eh? Five quid?'

'You're on.'

'I won't come out, Alec. Might attract attention. Be seeing you.'

Vine walked quickly to the van, climbed up, and pulled the door to. At once, the driver began to move away.

'Ah, Mr. Vine, we meet again.'

Seated at the far end was Professor Abraham Cornfeld.

CHAPTER TEN

Vine could not keep the surprise from his face.

'Hallo, professor. I didn't think we'd meet again.'

Cornfeld motioned towards the driver, indicating that they should speak with caution.

'Mr. Appleton thought that as long as transport was already organised, I might as well share with you. Save the taxpayers' money, eh?'

'Oh, every time.'

There was more to this than a feeble story like that, Vine decided. Still, it would have to wait until they were not overheard.

'Do you live in the area, professor?'

'For the moment, yes. I have a married sister here, and such time as I ever spend in one place, I stay with her. My work takes me all over, so I couldn't really claim to live anywhere, not in any permanent sense.'

Of course, Vine remembered. Deputy Chief Appleton had said the man was a special consultant to the Associated Northern Universities. There were quite a few of those, so he must be chasing all over the place. One day here, a couple there, probably no settled period in any one spot. No kind of life, the policeman decided. It might sound all very exciting, to people with routine eight-hour days in office or factory, but the reality would not be very acceptable. A strange bed every other night, nothing to call your own. No, it wouldn't do.

'Must be quite a busy life,' he said, lamely.

'There's enough to do,' agreed his companion. 'The difficulty is, I haven't any time for a hobby, and I would like that. Are you a gardener, or a stamp collector or something, Mr. Vine?'

Vine shook his head.

'Same problem as yourself, professor. Different reason, of course. I manage to live in one place, but being a copper, I don't see much of it. Have to do the garden of course, but only enough to keep the neighbours from complaining.'

After that, they lapsed into silence, each preoccupied with his own thoughts as the riot van bumped its unsprung way into the city. They slowed to a halt at a busy junction, and the driver spoke for the first time.

'Hope you gentlemen won't mind, but I'll have to drop you off at the back of the station, in the railway police yard. It wouldn't do to let

131

the public see what kind of bread we deliver.'

'Quite understand, driver,' Vine replied.

The professor didn't bother to answer, and a few minutes later they stopped again. The driver climbed out of his seat, and soon there was a scraping at the rear doors, and he stood smiling at them.

'Here we are then. If you would like to go through that gate there,' and he pointed, 'it brings you into the rear of the station.'

Vine climbed out, thanking him, and stood waiting for Cornfeld. The professor followed him, and Vine noticed the suitcase for the first time.

'Are you catching the train as well?' he queried. Cornfeld smiled sadly.

'I'm never doing anything else,' he replied. 'Shall we see if there's time for a cup of coffee, before we go our ways?'

'Good idea.'

They walked into the station, past the busy G.P.O. area, where great trolley-loads of parcels shunted back and forth, into some mysterious semblance of order.

'Superintendent, I wonder whether you would mind if I were to ask you to catch a later train?'

Here it comes, thought Vine.

'Well, er, bit difficult professor. My people will expect me back on duty the moment I'm finished up here.'

The blue eyes stared at him gravely.

132

'Quite. But the thing is, you see, you are not finished yet. Not quite. There is the question of our talk, yours and mine.'

'My Chief Constable—'

'—has been told to expect you when he sees you,' finished Cornfeld decisively.

Vine blinked. He had heard correctly, he supposed. This man had said 'told'. The chief constable had been 'told'. In his world, people didn't tell chief constables. They were the ones who told people.

'Well, of course, if you're sure it'll cause no trouble,' he muttered unhappily.

'None at all, I assure you. My sister's house is empty at this hour. We could have our chat there. It's only a few minutes away. We'll get a taxi.'

The house sat well back from a pleasant, tree-lined avenue. Vine took in the well-kept lawns, and the mock-Tudor building, glowing under the winter sun. Could be in the middle of Surrey, he thought.

'Not exactly everyone's image of Manchester,' he commented.

Cornfeld grinned.

'Well, it can't rain all the time, you know,' he gibed. 'The law of averages has to operate, even up here.'

Inside, they settled into comfortable chairs, and Vine accepted the offer of a drink.

'Plenty of water, please,' he requested.

Abe Cornfeld opted for soda, and they

133

saluted each other.

'Cheers.'

'Mr. Vine, I suggest we get right to it. This murder investigation of yours, it is really a matter of passing interest only. To me, that is. I appreciate that it's very much more to you.'

The superintendent was puzzled.

'Well, then?' he began.

'Well then, what is this all about?' anticipated the other. 'First, let me deal with the murders. There is little doubt in my mind that the man you want is an unbalanced type of person. If you don't find him quickly he will kill again. In fact, speaking entirely as an outsider, I fancy he will go on until he is apprehended. A dreadful, sordid business, but very much a police matter. Very much routine, and I'm certain he will be caught in the end.'

I wish I could feel as confident, thought Vine privately. These unpredictables were the very worst kind to track down.

Cornfeld had paused, to give him a chance to reply, but there seemed to be nothing useful to say.

'Yes, you will catch him, I am sure of it,' he resumed. 'My interest here is in you, Mr. Vine. Your report of the Great Bravington murder was what sparked me off. You spoke personally, and at length, with this creature. The one who called himself Nosferatu.'

Creature. That was what he'd said. Vine nodded.

134

'Yes. I was some time with him,' he agreed.

'Or it,' supplemented the professor. 'Oh yes, you are surprised. Naturally so, but not more than I was, when I first read your report. It was a most odd experience. I was reading a solid, factual police report, indeed, if you will forgive me, it was almost dull. Then I came to the interview with Nosferatu, and I had a curious experience. Although the flow of words was much the same, I could detect something in the mind of the man who wrote them. I read it again, with great care, to be certain I was not mistaken. Behind the words, behind the facts, a carefully unemotional presentation of detail, there was a withdrawal, a detachment even more complete than is normal. It took me a while to realise what caused it. But once I had identified the feeling, I had to know more. At first I thought it was fear, but I was wrong. It went much deeper. It was dread, Mr. Vine.'

The listener did not attempt to hide his astonishment.

'But I wrote and rewrote that a dozen times,' he protested. 'The first draft made me sound like an old lady walking down a dark street. I was sure I'd eliminated everything.'

'Everything but the atmosphere,' Cornfeld assured him. 'I became very curious. I wanted to know more about you, and it wasn't hard to learn. You are a brave man, superintendent. Your record speaks for itself on the point, and there are a number of people who will also speak for you, in that direction. So, I found myself saddled with an enigma. A senior police officer, with a long and distinguished career, confronted suddenly with a situation which brought this strong reaction. To be honest with you, it was the first spark of interest the case had produced from me. When Hap Appleton asked me to look at it, I did it without enthusiasm, believe me. But suddenly, it was as though the case came to life. I had to know more about Nosferatu, and I had to talk to you. Your witness Mr. James gave an address where Nosferatu could be contacted. The address did not appear in the report.'

Vine heaved his shoulders.

'There was no point. It turned out to be a phoney.'

'Ah. So Mr. James misled you?'

'Not deliberately. You can be sure I checked that most thoroughly. No, he gave me what he had. It was just a false lead, that's all.'

Cornfeld stroked at his golden beard.

'May I ask in what sense it was false? Are you saying that some perfectly innocent people occupied the place?'

'No. Worse than that. There was no such place.' The professor arched his eyebrows enquiringly, clearly waiting for more.

'The street existed all right,' continued Vine, 'but the numbers ended long before the number we had. It's an old trick.'

'And the Metropolitan Police will have been

most thorough, I am quite certain. Or are we, perhaps, in this instance, dealing with the City of London force?'

Vine started. Not many outsiders appreciated the distinction which had to be drawn between the two forces. To the world at large, a copper was a copper. Still, he reminded himself, there were quite a few things about this chap that set him a little apart from the world at large.

'Yes, it was the City people,' he confirmed. 'How did you know that?'

The deep eyes seemed almost to twinkle.

'I did not know it,' admitted the listener. 'I hoped it. Indeed, I find myself almost afraid to ask my next question, because I have high hopes of that one, also.'

Vine didn't think it was a time for games.

'Perhaps I'd better hear it,' he suggested, not quite tartly.

Cornfeld was not offended.

'The street in the City, what was it called please?'

The policeman opened his case, and riffled through papers.

'Here it is,' he announced. 'Wallock Street. Down by the river somewhere. I'm not an expert on London, I'm afraid. Ten minutes' walk away from Piccadilly Circus, and I'm lost.'

But the professor was not listening. He had expelled a low whistle of satisfaction, and was now prowling about the room. It was as though he'd forgotten Vine's presence.

Rum sort of bloke, decided the watching man. Got a bit remote sometimes, these scholar types. He'd stopped by the window now, and was staring out into the garden, where a group of starlings strutted around, looking for the final tidbits of the day.

'Great heavens, look at the time. I must go at once.'

'Go, professor?'

'Yes. I am addressing a meeting this evening in Dundee. A long-standing arrangement, which I could not possibly break. It'll have to wait until tomorrow.'

It was by no means clear to Vine what it was that would have to wait.

'You mean the case, professor?'

'No, no. Not quite. My television appearance.'

Vine sighed. Perhaps the man was the traditional potty professor after all.

'Oh,' he said politely. 'I hadn't realised you were going to be on the box.'

'Yes, yes, I think I ought to. One of these current affairs programmes will be best. Too many people stop watching the news, once they've heard the headlines.'

The man was speaking as though he had the right to walk into the studio and announce what time he'd decided to appear. Vine had no knowledge of the inner workings of television planning, but he doubted whether it would be quite that simple.

'You're not exactly scheduled, then?' he queried politely.

'What? Scheduled? No, of course not. But I think it's probably necessary. I'll decide in the morning.'

'You'll excuse me, professor, but will it be quite as simple as that? I thought all these things were controlled very tightly, and well in advance?'

Cornfeld looked at him then, the faint beginning of a smile hovering at the corners of his mouth.

'Controlled? Oh, yes, naturally. By people, Mr. Vine. And there are occasions, if it seems to be justified, when those people, in turn, have to be controlled. However, we shall see.'

Vine wondered again about his strange host. There was a lot more to this fellow than a rather pleasant appearance. For the moment, it seemed, the case had been put to one side. He got to his feet.

'Well, if there's nothing further then—' he began.

'Further? I should think there is. We've hardly started. Look, I have a place near King's Cross station. Kind of half a flat and half an office. Could you be there the day after tomorrow, please? At four o'clock in the afternoon.'

He scribbled the address on a piece of paper and held it out. Vine took it, shaking his head.

'My chief constable—' he muttered doubtfully.

'—will raise no difficulties,' finished Cornfeld crisply. 'Now then, I must grab my papers, and be off. Let me drop you at the station, Mr. Vine. What sort of library have you in your town?'

Library. It was really very difficult to keep the mind switching from subject to subject.

'Oh, very good. Very keen chap there.'

'Splendid. See if you can get hold of Kessel's "Peoples of the Danube". First class piece of work. Excellent man, Kessel.'

Vine capitulated.

'I'd better write it down.'

CHAPTER ELEVEN

The telephone shrilled.

Emma Vine stirred at once, groaned softly, and opened one eye to stare at the hazy green hands of the clock. Ye gods. Was that five-fifteen or twenty-five past three? What did it matter anyway? The night's sleep was ruined. What was needed, desperately needed, was a much larger clock, she decided. And a much quieter telephone. Why didn't Alec answer the blasted thing?

'Alec.'

'M'm.'

She knew that 'm'm'. It was one of his 'yes, dear, I shall deal with it at the first opportunity' kind of m'ms.

'Alec.'

This time she jabbed her elbow into the sleeping back. Vine grunted with irritation. Elbows meant telephones, his subconscious reminded him. He was reaching out for the instrument before his emerging mind actually registered the sound.

'Hallo.'

'Is that you, Mr. Vine? Superintendent Vine?'

The voice was familiar, but his head was not yet clear enough for identification work.

'Just a minute.'

Resting the phone on the night-table, he levered himself upright, shaking the night-fog from his head.

'Close your eyes, love.'

His wife screwed up her eyes against the sudden light from the bedside lamp.

'Hallo yes, this is Vine.'

'Cornfeld,' announced the intruder. 'We shall have to change our plans, I'm afraid.'

Change the plans. He was to meet the professor at the King's Cross address at four o'clock that afternoon. That was the only plan he knew.

'I see,' he returned vaguely.

'Yes, there's been a development. Our

141

friend has been at it again.'

All traces of sleep vanished instantly.

'Where?'

'In Glasgow. I'm calling from there now. I can't talk about it on the telephone. I think you should be up here, Mr. Vine.'

Up there? Glasgow? Ridiculous.

'I don't see how I—' he began.

'Tell me please,' the professor cut in, 'where is your nearest football ground?'

Football ground? The man was clearly off his chump. Or drunk.

'Foster Park,' he replied. 'But—'

'Foster Park. Good. How far is that from where you live?'

'Mile and a half. No, say two miles.'

'Splendid. Let us see, hold on a moment.'

There was muttering at the other end, as the professor conferred with someone. Then he spoke again.

'We shall need a little time to arrange things. Could you be at Foster Park in one hour's time?'

One hour. Vine picked up his watch and stared at it in disbelief.

'Do you know what time it is? It's three-thirty in the morning.'

There was a clucking noise.

'Good heavens, can it be true? Yes, yes, you are right. Things have been moving so quickly up here that I rather lost track. Three-thirty. Then, shall we say four forty-five at this park?

A helicopter will meet you.'

There was no point in arguing. The professor was not discussing possibilities with him. He was simply completing arrangements towards a pre-decided conclusion. Vine was about to leave for Glasgow, and there the matter ended.

'Helicopter, yes,' he repeated dully. He'd never been in one before.

'Splendid. I'll get a couple of hours sleep while you're on the way. See you at breakfast then.'

Vine found himself propped against the pillows, staring at the receiver, listening to the insistent buzzing sound.

'Alec, put it down, there's a love. It's making a hell of a row. Besides, supposing some more of your nice friends want to call? They can't get through while it's off the hook.'

'Sorry.'

Reaching out, he replaced the instrument. The noise ceased.

'Lovely man. Now, that yellow thing that's hurting our eyes is called the light. You'll find a switch by your hand, which turns it off.'

Pushing back the bedclothes, he swung reluctant feet towards the floor. His wife looked around then.

'Alec?'

'Sorry about the light. I'll be as quick as I can. I have to go to Glasgow. No need for you to get up.'

But she was already on the move, looking around for slippers. Emma Vine had been a policeman's wife too long to be difficult about a little thing like losing most of a night's sleep. Did he say Glasgow?

'You did say Glasgow, didn't you? I'll bet it's something to do with your crazy professor friend.'

Vine was rubbing at his cheek, wondering whether he really needed to shave at such an hour.

'Do you think I need a shave?'

He turned towards her for inspection.

'Not really. You know how sore it makes your face if there isn't enough beard. I should leave it a few hours.'

'H'm,' he said uncertainly. 'Don't want to look scruffy up there.'

Emma smiled to herself. Normally a man of quick decision, very much on the ball, her husband was always a little slow to gather himself when he was disturbed in the middle of the night. That was something about Superintendent Alec Vine which no one else but she knew.

'I'm sure, if you ask the local coppers nicely, there'll be a secret supply of hot water somewhere in Glasgow.'

'Good idea. I'll take a razor with me. And speaking of hot water—'

She nodded, making for the door.

'Tea or coffee?'

'Coffee, I think.'

He opened the wardrobe, lifting out an overnight bag. Five minutes later, after an invigorating wash, he was getting dressed as Emma returned with two steaming mugs.

'You were muttering something about a helicopter, just now. What was that about?'

Vine pulled the knot of his tie into place.

'Meeting me,' he explained. 'I'm going up in one.'

His wife sat on the bed, sipping at the coffee.

'You know I'm not too bright at this hour,' she said carefully. 'But what is this all about? Why Glasgow, and who was that on the phone, and why the helicopter, and about forty-three other questions that spring readily to mind?'

'Blimey, this is hot.' He set down the mug. 'New murder up there. Cornfeld says it's the same chap. Wants me up there with him.'

Strange, reflected Emma. This professor was supposed to be some kind of university lecturer. Thinking back to her own student days, she could recall an astonishing variety of talents among the faculty. Influences too, in some unexpected quarters. But she could not imagine any instance of someone who would be able to conjure up a helicopter in the middle of the night. Someone who seemed to be able to pull a senior police officer away from his home force with impunity.

Keeping incredulity out of her tone she

asked.

'I know you're a very good copper and all that, but why you, Alec? The last I heard, they had quite a few of their own policemen in Glasgow.'

Vine nodded. Not a man to underestimate his own qualities, he appreciated nevertheless the truth of what she was saying. The people up there most certainly had no need of his help as a policeman. Indeed, if that were the basis of the summons, he could probably look forward to a chilly reception, at best. But it wasn't that, he knew. It was because of the man Nosferatu. Creature, rather. That had been the way Cornfeld described him. And, looking at his wife's enquiring face, he knew he wasn't going to tell her. A few minutes before, in the bathroom, even as he splashed hot soapy water against his face, he had felt a sudden icy probe at the base of his spine. For a brief instant, he had recalled the presence in that room at the golf club, and the prospect that he may be going to face a similar experience. It was something he could not, would not, explain to the waiting Emma.

'Blessed if I know,' he shrugged. 'You heard my end of the conversation. I'm wanted up there, and that's all about it.'

'I see.'

He was lying, of course. Well, being evasive, at the very least. But Emma knew this was not a time to be pressing him. It was a time to be

146

ensuring he'd packed a toothbrush. And getting herself dressed, of course. She would have to drive him, because she had no intention of being left without a car while he was away.

Thirty minutes later, she drove past the rickety wooden terracing that had been constructed by the handful of supporters of the local football club. The car headlights picked out the ungainly intruder squatting in the middle of the pitch.

'Those things never look safe to me. No wings,' she complained. 'Are you sure you'll be all right?'

Before her husband could answer, there was a tap at the side window. She turned to see a man looking in. He seemed to be in some kind of uniform.

'Mr. Vine?'

'That's me.'

Alec leaned across and kissed her on the cheek.

'I don't know how long this will take, love. I'll phone you when I know what the form is.'

Climbing out, he looked at the waiting man.

'Army?' he questioned. 'I didn't know the military were involved.'

'Always glad to oblige the law,' grinned the other. 'In any case, this is a very useful night training exercise.'

That didn't sound very reassuring.

'Training?' echoed the superintendent. 'You

mean I'm going up with a learner?'

'Lord, no. No L-plates, if that's worrying you. But we don't get many opportunities to do a blind night pick-up like this. No ground lights, you see.'

As a reassurance, it was going to have to suffice.

*   *   *

Hours later, he leaned back from a plate now clean of the sizzling eggs and bacon, and looked across the table at Cornfeld, who had newly arrived.

'Morning professor. Thanks for letting me finish my breakfast. What's the form here?'

Cornfeld smiled, stroking at his little beard. He liked this man Vine.

'Murder, Mr. Vine. There can be no doubt we are dealing with the same man. It was really most fortunate that I should be relatively close at hand. We are able to be on the scene, as it were, more or less at the outset.'

Vine used up time searching for his cigarettes and lighting one. The matter of the professor's presence in Scotland had been occupying his mind during the trip in the helicopter. It could be no more than a fortunate coincidence. On the other hand, the previous crime had been committed in Manchester, where he lived. And there was no denying the man's great interest in the subject, nor his obviously detailed knowledge of it. On top of that, there was the question of how he came to be on the scene so fast. Exhaling smoke, he replied,

'Yes. That was a bit of luck, certainly. How did you come to get wind of it so quickly, professor?'

The younger man chuckled, well aware of his companion's thought-processes.

'Scarcely luck, superintendent. A rather simple matter of administration, in fact, You see, all chief constables have been circularised, and I am to be contacted the moment such a crime is detected. In turn, I have to advise my movements.'

Vine digested this new information. It seemed to eliminate his half-formed suspicions, only to replace them with a larger question. The question of who this man was. No ordinary university professor, that much was clear. It took more than that kind of authority to drag the army out of bed in the middle of the night, and to speak calmly of circularising all chief constables. For the moment, decided Vine, he would do better to stick to the job in hand.

'The local people know I'm here, of course?'

'Oh, yes. But you are not here as a police officer. It makes things smoother all round if you appear simply as my—er—colleague. I have told them you have been detached from

149

your post for this purpose. It eliminates any little worries about protocol and so forth. You will be quite well received, I assure you.'

Colleague, reflected the listener. With a pause before the word, the pause being just long enough to substitute 'colleague' for 'assistant'.

'Well then, I'd better know who I'm supposed to be working for, hadn't I?'

Cornfeld dismissed the subject with a small flutter of the hand.

'You will not be questioned, Mr. Vine. You may be assured of that. Your authority here will be in no doubt. Now tell me, did you manage to read that book I recommended?'

' "Peoples of the Danube"? Yes, I've got it in my bag, but I've hardly started to read it. I had thought there'd be a little more time.'

'Try to work it in on the way to London. There will be several hours free.'

London was still on, then.

'You think we'll be finished here today?'

'I hope so. But you must be the judge. As I have already explained to you, I have no great interest in the police aspects of this matter, you are the expert, and I leave all that side to you.' The professor looked at his watch. 'They will be ready for us in fifteen minutes. It will take us most of that to drive to the meeting. If you are ready then, Mr. Vine?'

The meeting was a brisk, business-like affair. Vine met the chief super in charge of the case, and the inspector from the local division. If they resented the intrusion from outside, they managed to conceal the fact very carefully, and presented the facts in a straightforward professional manner.

The pattern was depressingly familiar.

The victim was a young schoolmistress, Helen Parsons, aged twenty-three. The annual fund-raising event for her school had been held on the previous evening, in the form of an Old-Time Music Hall evening. There had been a stage show, with parents and staff presenting a variety programme, followed by dancing. All those attending had worn period costume, and on hearing this Vine exchanged glances with Cornfeld.

'Men aren't usually very good at this sort of thing,' he pointed out. 'They usually settle for curly moustaches and straw boaters. Or dinner jackets with plenty of medals. Was that the case here?'

'Inspector?'

The officer in charge looked at the local man, who nodded.

'Broadly speaking, sir. One or two people hired military uniforms but otherwise it was much as Mr. Vine suggests.'

'Thank you. Please carry on.'

There had been plenty to drink throughout the entire evening, and people were vague about precise details as time wore on. With a crowd of over four hundred, many of them visitors, no one was able to give a very clear picture of events around midnight. It was fairly well established that the man who called himself the Count had not been present during the early part of the festivities. The organisers had admitted that their ticket-checking arrangements, strictly followed at the beginning of the evening, had tailed away from nine o'clock onwards. By ten o'clock, there was no one really responsible, and it would have been a simple matter for a late arrival to mingle, unnoticed, with the crowd.

Helen Parsons had been a leading figure in the stage presentation, singing a few old ditties, and joining in the Can-Can. A vivacious, attractive girl, she had no shortage of partners once the dancing began. Witnesses were extremely vague as to when they first noticed her dancing with the stranger, the Count. A little after midnight, several people remembered them leaving the hall. The girl was very pale, and leaning heavily on the man's arm. He had explained quickly that she was feeling faint, and a few minutes in the fresh air would soon revive her.

No one saw her again, until she was found in a local park, an hour later. The details of the murder tallied exactly with the earlier cases. The scratch on her wrist, and a wooden stake driven through her heart.

But at least this time there were a number of people who could describe the man. There were variations in points of detail, but a fairly good picture had emerged.

'Enough for a photo-fit, inspector?'

'I would say so, yes.'

'Is there a picture of the girl?'

Vine looked at the latest victim, noting her luxuriant black hair.

'Professor?'

Cornfeld inclined his head.

'Yes, I have noticed. Tell me, inspector, did anyone happen to hear him address this unfortunate girl as Lucy?'

The inspector was puzzled.

'Lucy, sir? No. Or at least, it hasn't been brought to my attention. Girl's name was Helen. I don't quite follow, sir.'

The professor made a face of dismissal.

'It is not a matter of large importance. The man has an obsession with Lucy. But there is quite sufficient evidence that this is our man, without that final piece. Wouldn't you say so, Mr Vine?'

'Overwhelming, I'm afraid,' assented Vine.

The chief superintendent cleared his throat.

'I am instructed to place myself at your disposal in this case, Professor Cornfeld. What is the next step, please?'

He didn't like it, and Vine could well understand the way he must be feeling. It was to be hoped that the professor would deal with things delicately.

'I have not come here today to meddle in

153

police business, chief superintendent. Quite the reverse in fact. If you will be kind enough to let Mr. Vine see the body, and he may wish to interview a few of the witnesses, I think—' he looked enquiringly at Vine, who nodded— 'then I'm sure he will be able to supply you with a great deal of information which will help to speed up your investigations. As for myself, I have only to thank you for your courtesy and great patience in the way you have received us. After I have had a few words with my colleague—'

—there was that word again—

'—I shall leave you, and wish you every success in tracking down this madman. Alec, if you please.'

Vine followed him into the next room. Cornfeld closed the door.

'I haven't any doubts that this is our man. Have you?'

'No, professor. But just the same, I'd be happier if I could snoop around a bit more, get the feel of things. You see, with this kind of crime, something a bit out of the run, there's always a risk of imitators. Someone using the outward trappings of the same formula to commit a murder which they've been secretly planning anyway. I'd like to satisfy myself about that aspect.'

Cornfeld wasn't really paying him much attention. It was evident that he was finished here, and anxious to be off.

'Yes, I quite understand. Very wise precaution, I have no doubt. However, it is very much your concern, and an area in which I have no contribution to make. I must be off, there is much to be done. Could you try to be at the King's Cross place tonight, please? As soon after ten as possible?'

Vine looked at his watch.

'That'll mean leaving here by mid-afternoon,' he muttered. 'Yes, I'm sure I shall be through by then.'

'Excellent. Now, the book, Kessel's book. I realise that time is against you, and it's very difficult to stay awake in trains. But do try to read it. You'll understand so much better what we are up against. If you really can't manage all of it, concentrate on Chapters Three, Four and Eleven.'

'Three, Four and Eleven.'

'Yes. Oh, and do let these people have as much help as you possibly can. Stick to investigative procedures, and keep the other aspects out of it, if humanly possible. We don't want to spread a lot of ill-informed speculation.'

Vine shook his head.

'There's quite enough here to keep us coppers busy, without any of those—er—other aspects.' The professor was satisfied.

'Good. Then I'm off. I will see you tonight.'

And he was gone.

Vine stroked thoughtfully at his chin.

Mustn't forget about that shave.

CHAPTER TWELVE

Susan Duncan put down her suitcase and tapped at the staff nurse's door. A brisk, bright ginger-headed nurse looked up from her writing.

'Oh hallo, Mrs. Duncan. We're opening the gates, are we?'

Sue smiled.

'Yes, at last. You must be sick of the sight of me.'

The staff nurse shook her head.

'Don't you believe it. If all our patients were as little trouble, this job would be a bit easier. Anyway, we're all very relieved to see you recover. Three weeks is a long time. You're really very lucky there's no permanent damage.'

'Yes. I suppose so.'

'Now,' the nurse picked up a small yellow bottle. 'Don't forget, two of these before you go to bed. We've given you enough for four days, but I really don't think you'll need them all. If you find that you do, just let your own doctor know. And don't forget, an appointment has been made at your local hospital, three months from now. It's written on here. Just a final precaution.'

'Thank you, staff. Funny, but I'm a bit sorry to be going, really. Perhaps it's the peace and quiet.'

'You'd be surprised how many say that. Well, good luck. Someone picking you up?'

'Er, no. I'll take a taxi to the station. Goodbye, and thank you.'

As she turned to go, she met one of her favourite nurses on her way into the office.

'Goodbye, Margaret. Thanks for all you've done.'

'Goodbye Mrs. Duncan. Take care.'

Margaret stood and watched her as she left the ward.

'Funny business, that. Felt sorry for her.'

'Sorry?'

'Well, yes. I mean, you'd think her husband could have come to see her. Even just for five minutes. Or telephoned. He didn't even bother to find out whether she was alive or dead.'

The staff nurse nodded.

'More there than meets the eye. Mind you, you wouldn't expect him to be very pleased, would you? Car smash in the middle of the night, when she was out with another man.'

'No, I suppose not. Still, it seems hard.'

'Now, what about Mrs. Purdey? Is she ready for Doctor?'

They got back to work, and Sue Duncan went out of their minds.

Two hours later, her second taxi of the day

drew up outside her front door.

'One eighty-five, madam.'

She didn't respond at first, but stood staring at the outside of the house.

'Something wrong, madam?'

'Eh? Oh, no, I'm sorry. Thank you.'

She gave him two pound notes, and he went away. Feeling in her handbag, she found the key of the front door, and walked reluctantly up the path. Donald's car was missing, so it seemed he was away again. Just as well, she wanted a chance to settle herself in, before the questioning began. For there was no doubt she was in trouble, and equally there was no doubt it was entirely her own fault.

The door would not swing open at the first push. She shoved harder, and found it wide enough to permit her entrance. The obstruction had been caused by newspapers and post, which formed a great untidy heap on the mat. Her earlier reluctance was now overcome by puzzlement.

'Donald?' she shouted, then again.

The empty house waited around her. She dropped her suitcase, then walked into the kitchen. A few unwashed plates lay in the sink.

'Donald?'

She moved quickly to the other rooms downstairs, finding nothing. Then she began to climb the stairs, quickly at first, then more and more slowly. Her heart was pounding, and her mouth had gone dry. At the top, her voice was little more than a whisper.

'Donald?'

The empty bedrooms told her nothing. Outside her husband's room she stood, irresolute. The black padlock was firmly in place, swallowing hard, she tapped lightly at the door.

'Donald? It's me.'

There was no reply. She tried again, with the same result. It was clear that something was amiss. Donald had never stayed away longer than two days. Now, it must have been—the newspapers would tell her. Running downstairs, she gathered everything from the mat, dumping it on the dining-room table, and beginning to sort through.

The earliest newspaper was dated sixteen days before. She had been out of the house for three weeks, well, twenty days to be exact. So Donald had been at home since the accident, for at least four days. He had not been home since.

The mail.

Perhaps there was a letter from him. Some explanation. But there was nothing in his familiar slanted scrawl. There were two business letters addressed to him, postmarked from Manchester and Glasgow. Her first impulse was to open them, but Donald got so angry if she interfered with his business papers. It was possible that he'd left her, of course. More than possible, after what had happened. But not without a word, surely. Not without a row, some kind of inquisition about herself and Ian Paulson. Perhaps his boss would be able to help. Mr. Dalrimple. Yes, of course. He may not know anything about their domestic affairs, but at least he'd have some idea of where Donald might be. Or whether something had happened to him, perhaps. A car crash, a sudden illness. She had a note of the number somewhere, probably in the telephone table.

She found it eventually, and dialled. She could hear the brr-brr at the other end, but no one answered. It had been a remote hope anyway. It was almost one o'clock on a working day, and the nature of the job involved being out of the office most of the time. Even if it was an office number she was dialling, and not his home telephone.

Feeling frustrated as well as worried, she went into the kitchen and put a kettle on to boil. Stirring instant coffee into a mug, she went into the dining-room to sit down and think. Among the circulars and other post, she saw the two notes she'd written from the hospital. Both unopened. There was a glossy circular addressed to her from a cosmetics firm. Setting down the coffee, she glanced idly at a newspaper. 'Dracula Strikes in Manchester', announced the headline. She shuddered, and turned it over without reading. Try the telephone again.

Out in the hall she stood listening to the ringing tone for three clear minutes, before giving up hope. Then she went back to her coffee. The house had never felt so lonely and oppressive. She opened her handbag to find a cigarette, and lit it. After two puffs, she decided she didn't want it. Looking round for an ashtray, she realised it had been covered up with newspapers. She pushed them impatiently aside to find it. As she reached over to grind out the cigarette, another headline screamed at her. 'Glasgow's New Vampire Victim.'

Sue Duncan paused and looked for the other newspaper, the one she'd seen first. There it was. Manchester—Glasgow. She was beginning to imagine things. It was ridiculous of course. Donald moved all over the country. It was natural for him to get letters. But that room upstairs, those terrible things in it. With trembling hands, she picked up Donald's letters, and opened them. The first one said,

'Dear Mr Duncan,

With reference to your call at these offices yesterday—'

The other one began,

'Dear Sir,

I refer to our meeting here of today's date—'

Susan smoothed out the letters and placed them against the newspaper stories, comparing the dates. Donald Duncan had been in Manchester and in Glasgow on the dates the murders had been committed. She gave a low gasp, and clutched at the back of a chair, thinking back. She could not remember the date of the first murder, but she could recall it happening, quite clearly. Because on that night Donald had been away from home, and she had been—well, never mind that now. The point to remember was where he had been. Cambridge. That was it. Cambridge. And from Cambridge to Great Bravington couldn't be further than twenty or twenty-five miles. If only she could contact Mr. Dalrimple.

Her fingers refused at first to remain steady in the numbers of the dial. Finally she was successful, and the familiar ringing buzzed in her ear.

Police. She ought to go to the police. But supposing she was making a mountain out of a molehill? It would be so disloyal to Donald. Particularly if he was lying in hospital somewhere. Ill or injured. Well, all right. But surely that was a job for the police, anyway? Whichever way one looked at it, she argued, her husband was missing from home. Had been, for sixteen days. Surely that was long enough? They wouldn't put her down as an hysterical woman. Well, she decided at last, even if they did, she had to talk to somebody.

Picking up the telephone, she dialled the operator.

'I want the police, please.'

162

*　　*　　*

It was an hour later that the blue and white car pulled up outside the house, and a young police constable climbed out. Sue had changed her clothes, to shake off the last of the hospital, and spent some time on her appearance. Her mother had always said 'if your appearance goes, my girl, your morale goes with it.'

P.C. Evans was agreeably surprised by the attractive woman who answered the door.

'Mrs. Duncan?'

'Yes, please come in officer.'

He followed her into the sitting room, his eyes busy taking everything in.

'I'll have to ask you a number of questions, madam. With a Missing Person case, I'm afraid it's all necessary.'

'Yes, of course.' Sue was so delighted to see him that she didn't care how many questions he had. 'Please sit down.'

'Thank you.'

They began, and gradually Evans pieced together the explanation as to why it had taken so long for the missing husband to be brought to their notice.

'An industrial chemist, you say, madam. Could I have the name and address of his employers?'

'Well, he doesn't talk much about his work, but I believe they work on a sort of sub-agent basis for one of the large drug companies.'

'I see. You mentioned "they". Your husband has a partner, has he?'

'Not a partner, no. Mr. Dalrimple is his boss. Donald works for him.'

'Mr. Dalrimple, right.' Evans wrote it down. 'Is that with a "y"?'

'No. With an "i".'

'Right. Initials?'

Sue checked the handwritten note she'd made.

'A.V.'

There were many more questions. The young policeman had not been exaggerating about that. Finally he seemed satisfied.

'Now madam. Two more things. Have you a recent photograph of your husband?'

'Not a good one. Not a studio portrait, if that's what you mean.'

'Anything. Holiday snap will do. So long as it's a good likeness.'

'Yes. I'm sure I can find something.'

'Thank you. Last thing then. I'm afraid I have to search the house.'

Her eyes widened.

'Search the house? Quite unnecessary, believe me. He's not here. I've looked everywhere.'

Have you, love? he wondered. Have you checked he hasn't hanged himself behind one of the doors? Blown out his brains in the loft? Poisoned himself and hidden under a bench in the shed, to die? But aloud, he said, 'I'm sure you have, madam. And I'm sure I'll find nothing. It's just part of the routine. I have to do it.'

She hesitated.

'Just one thing. There's one room my husband always keeps locked. From outside. It's locked now. I have no key, I'm afraid.'

The police officer frowned.

'I'm sorry madam, but I'll have to effect entry. That's exactly the sort of situation we have to watch out for, in a case like this.'

'But, as I say, there's no key,' she protested. Not very strongly.

He stood up.

'I'll fetch a screwdriver from the car, madam. I'll try to avoid damage.'

Five minutes later he was turning at the last screw holding the hasp to the door.

'I think it would be better if I go in alone, madam, if you don't mind.'

The hasp swung clear, and the doorknob turned in his hand. In you go, Evans, he instructed himself. He swung the door wide, and stepped inside.

'Good grief,' he muttered.

There was no sign of Donald Duncan, but there was quite enough to spark off the imagination of a bright young officer.

'I'll have to ask for the use of your telephone, madam,' he said firmly.

CHAPTER THIRTEEN

Alec Vine was tired. Hauled from his bed at three-thirty in the morning, he had been on duty continuously ever since, and it was now approaching ten o'clock at night. Even on the train, when he might reasonably have hoped to nod off for an hour or two, he'd had his compulsory reading to do. Still, he had to admit to himself, the professor had known what he was about when he recommended the book.

Doctor Kessel may have set out to produce a work of scholarship, and for all Vine could judge, he probably had succeeded. But he had inadvertently written at the same time a masterly backdrop to the murder investigations now in progress.

'Is this it, guv?'

The taxi-driver's voice cut across his thinking. He stared out of the window at an unprepossessing tobacconist's shop front.

'I don't know,' he replied. 'Never been here before.'

The driver sighed.

'It's the number you gave me.'

Vine climbed out and walked across the pavement. A battered door separated the tobacconist from the next shop, and he could just make out the rusty metal numbers.

166

Returning to the cab, he nodded.

'This is it. Thank you.'

He paid the fare, and a few seconds later he was alone on the ill-lit street. The scarred door was innocent of any bell-push or knocker. About to pound on it with his fist, Vine changed his mind and tried the handle. It turned, and he found himself staring up a worn stairway, lit by a solitary fly-specked bulb. There was a sudden rush of movement, and something brushed against his legs. Vine started, then saw a bundle of black fur land with a soft thud halfway up the stairs. An ill-favoured cat stared at him with yellow eyes.

'Steady on mog,' he muttered. 'You made me jump.'

He began to mount upwards, and the cat turned at once to lead the way. At the top, there was a door on the right hand side. The cat sat, waiting. Vine rapped at the door. There was a crackling sound above his head, and a distorted voice asked,

'Who is it, please?'

'It's me, professor. Alec Vine.'

After a brief wait, the door opened. A man in his late twenties grinned at him cheerfully.

'You made good time, Mr. Vine. It's only nine forty-five. Please come in. And you found Stalin, too. Wondered where he'd got to.'

The cat had already disappeared inside. Vine stepped in. The other man held out his hand.

'Frank Weston,' he announced. 'I'm sort of general dogsbody around here. Let me take your coat, Mr. Vine.'

His handshake was firm and dry. Vine shrugged out of his overcoat. They were standing in a small hallway, with two doors leading off.

'Thank you.' What did the chap mean, 'general dogsbody'? Doing what? 'I've beaten the professor to it, have I?'

'Yes, he won't be here for some time I'm afraid. Shall we go inside?'

Weston led him into a large room, which seemed to be undecided as to whether it was an office or someone's living quarters. There was an ancient desk, two filing cabinets, one small table complete with typewriter; also, one settee, one armchair, and a bed. The far corner of the room was given over to a powerful array of electronic equipment, some of which was familiar to Vine, but the rest was a mystery.

His young host chuckled.

'Bit rum at first inspection, isn't it? Do people live here, work here, or play mad scientists? Spot of each really. That's my department over there. I'm what you might call the professor's pet gadgeteer. Would you like some coffee?'

Vine was still somewhat bemused by the bizarre surroundings.

'Eh? Oh yes. Thank you.'

He sat down, feeling for cigarettes as Weston went out. What was it the professor had said, 'a sort of flat'? Something like that.

'Here we are. Hope you don't mind mugs.'

The coffee was surprisingly good. Vine sipped at it, and set down his mug.

'You said the professor would be some time. Could you be more specific?'

The young man shook his head.

'Not much. He's very good about times, really. Left to himself, he'd never be late anywhere. But so many people are chasing him all the time, with one thing and another, that he can't call his soul his own. But we'll be seeing him in a few minutes.' Then, noting the puzzlement brought about this last statement, he added quickly 'on the box. Television. He's going to be on Headline Tuesday at ten fifteen.'

'Is he, by George. He muttered something about an appearance, but he didn't give me any details.'

'The times I've heard people say that,' sighed the young man. 'He's not a great one for explanations, at times. Have you been mugging up on "Peoples of the Danube", Kessel's book?'

Vine was startled by the question.

'Why yes. Or that is, I've had a couple of hours at it.'

'Then I'm ahead of you. I've had most of the day to get myself clued up. The professor suggested we might sort of compare notes, if you've no objection. Seemed to think it might be a help to both of us.

The superintendent opened his case and removed his copy of the book.

'I've only concentrated on certain chapters,' he announced. 'Wouldn't fancy my chances for an "O" level.'

'Nor I. Still, let's see if we have the same general understanding. Oh, and I haven't bothered much with dates. Kessel says in the introduction that a lot of the source material conflicts with itself within twenty or thirty years.'

'Yes, and the text bears him out. But it's fairly clear the story starts in mid-fifteenth century.'

Weston began stuffing black tobacco into a well-charred pipe.

'The part we're concerned with, yes. In the country they used to call Wallachia. There was the usual crop of local wars, landgrabbers, cruel barons and the rest of it. Every few years, the locals would get brassed off and have some kind of uprising. When you read about the conditions they lived under, you could hardly blame the poor sods.'

Vine agreed.

'Yes, but as I understand it, the really big struggle, the one that mattered, was the power game between the Turks and the forces of Islam on the one hand, and the Eastern

Christian Empire on the other. All the local states were dragged in at one time or another, and one of those to suffer was Wallachia. The Christians had established several monasteries, and the monks were doing their best, but they had no immunity so far as the local barons were concerned. They were just as liable to be attacked or tortured as any other members of the community.'

Weston puffed a thick cloud towards the ceiling.

'Which brings us to the man called Ferdinand of Targovisti. He got a band of monks together, and decided to clear off. Make a big pilgrimage to Vienna. That was the cover story. In fact, what they were doing was emigrating. The bulk of the party were plain peasants, about two hundred of them. Whole families. It wasn't the first time that kind of escape had been tried. The usual drill was to let them get about fifty miles, well away from any large town, then quietly butcher the lot. But for some reason which even Kessel can't explain, this mob got away, with it. Which brings us right to the crunch of our particular story.'

Vine leaned forward.

'You mean the soil.'

'The soil, precisely. The earth was the source of life. These people were not going to be parted from it. They took it with them. By the cartload. Good Lord, look at the time.'

171

The policeman looked at his watch. As he did so, the door buzzer sounded. Weston went out, and came back with Professor Cornfeld.

'So sorry Frank, I seem to have mislaid my key.'

'Again,' groaned Weston.

Vine got to his feet.

'Hallo professor.'

'Ah, Mr. Vine. Has Frank been looking after you?' Cornfeld's tone was pleasant as always, but he seemed somehow abstracted.

'Yes,' Vine confirmed. 'We've been comparing notes about Kessel's book.'

'Good, good, that will save us some time. Frank, could we have the television on please? I should be about due now.'

Weston tuned in the set, and Cornfeld hung his coat on the back of the door. Then he picked up Weston's coffee and drank some.

'Good,' he observed. 'Right, let's get comfortable. I had to get quite short with the television people to get this broadcast tonight. We'd better see how it comes over.'

Vine found that his surprise at the awesome authority wielded by this man was lessening with each new experience.

'Think it'll do any good, professor?' he asked tentatively.

Cornfeld sighed. 'I hope so, I really hope so. Certainly it will do no harm. The public at large will have a much better understanding of what is going on. But that is an incidental

172

benefit. The main thing is for our murderer to know that we're on to him.'

'He may not know it's on, of course,' suggested Vine hesitantly.

'True, but we've done all we can. The show's been referred to on every newscast, television and radio, for the past two hours. If our chap doesn't know, he'll be the only one in the country. Think we could run to some more coffee, Frank, while we're watching this?'

They shifted their chairs into position, while the final stages of a football match were played out. Then the familiar opening music came up, and the show began. The interviewer's face was very grave.

'Vampire,' he said with relish, 'a word that has struck terror into our hearts for five hundred years. Never more so than today.'

He went on about the series of murders, with particular emphasis on the latest victim whose body had been found only a few hours earlier. Vine was especially interested in these fragments. After that, the programme turned its attention to the vampire in fiction. There were clips from old movies, including some rare footage from the great German classic, Nosferatu. Vine leaned forward at the mention of the name, fascinated. This was followed by some rather obvious time-filling. Then the presenter filled the screen with his most solemn face.

'So much, then, for the myth. But what is

myth, and what is fact? To most of us, the two seem inextricably woven together. But tonight, we are fortunate to have with us in the studio Professor Abraham Cornfeld . . .'

He went on about Cornfeld's various official appointments, and finally the professor himself appeared. The interviewer asked Cornfeld a few questions. They were unimportant, and served mainly to loosen up the professor in front of the cameras.

'This prince, Vlad Tepes, sometimes called Vlad the Impaler. Could you tell us more about him?'

'Yes.' Cornfeld smoothed his silky beard and spoke directly to the camera. Vine felt a momentary superiority over his fellow-watchers. He'd heard this stuff before, or most of it. The professor repeated most of the information he'd given to the police conference in Manchester, then moved on to some new information, something about a monk leading an exodus from the country, which Vine had heard previously.

'An epic journey indeed,' intoned Cornfeld.

'That is quite clear from what you have told us, professor. I'm sure we could use up the rest of our time quite easily, talking on this point alone. But unfortunately we have to press on. Tell us something about the end of the journey.'

Weston leaned forward, listening intently. The professor seemed slightly huffed to have the mammoth expedition dismissed so quickly.

'Very well,' he said grudgingly. 'I will gloss over the hardships of those unfortunate people. They were hounded at every step. People did not want them, at any stage of the journey. They were labelled as devil-worshippers, and moved on. In the last stages of desperation, and some two years after leaving their homeland, they arrived on the coast of France. From there, they took ship to England. They arrived in London, either in 1457 or 1458, and there they settled.'

The interviewer interrupted.

'You said earlier, professor, that they started out with cartloads of their native soil. Was that still the case, after all those tribulations?'

'Oh yes. It is listed in the ship's inventory. It's all quite clear.'

The interviewer looked patronising.

'It was five hundred years ago, professor. Can we really be as precise as all that?'

But Cornfeld was not to be ruffled.

'Very much more precise, if necessary. The authoritative source of reference on the history of London is Professor John Haldwell's Notes on Mediaeval London, a most scholarly work in three volumes. There is a mine of useful—and reliable' he emphasised maliciously 'information about the landing of the Wallachian party. The consignment of earth is clearly recorded. And of course, the evidence of the little settlement is far more up to date, and available to anyone who cares to go and look.'

He paused, to provoke the inevitable question.

'What evidence is that, professor?'

'They stayed together, in the new country. In exactly the same way that groups of migrants always have, and always will. The City of London soon absorbed them, and the exact site is that of a street named after them hundreds of years ago. It was called Wallack Street, originally, but with the passing of the years it became gradually anglicised. It's still there, in the City, down by the Thames. Nowadays, we know it as Wallock Street, E.C.1.'

'The facts seem to be irrefutable.'

'Totally,' said Cornfeld smugly.

But the presenter was an old hand, and his composure remained.

'Now professor, I know that you, as an historian, deal in facts, and I will not attempt to lead you on matters of fiction. But in the early part of this programme, we did establish that all popular fiction is agreed that a vampire must return to his own soil, to rest.'

'Such is the legend, I can say no more.'

'Quite. But if we could just remain with that point for a moment, you are saying that such soil exists, in this country. In Wallock Street, to be exact.'

'I am.'

'So therefore, it is true to say that there is a natural resting place for a vampire, in the heart of our capital city.'

'There's one other thing—' began the professor.

'I'm sorry professor, but we have run out of time.' The presenter stared into the camera, and the low, eerie music began to wail behind his voice. 'And there' he said menacingly 'are the facts. The facts this—'

'That is a pity. Turn it off, Frank.'

Cornfeld scowled, and stood up.

'What's the matter? Didn't they do as you asked?' queried Weston.

'Most of it, yes. But I wanted the murderer to know we're onto him from the poison angle. Might have driven him to a mistake.'

The telephone rang. Weston picked it up, and listened. His eyes grew bright, and he pointed urgently at the instrument with his free hand. Cornfeld waited. So did the superintendent. Finally, Weston said 'thank you' and replaced the receiver.

'It's all over, bar the shouting. They know who he is.'

'The devil they do. Speak up man, what's the story?'

'His name is Donald Duncan, age 31. Industrial chemist, as we had wondered. Been missing for the past sixteen days. Known to have been in Glasgow and Manchester on the crucial dates. Also, superintendent, he was in

177

Cambridge on the night of your murder.'

'Close enough,' nodded Vine.

'You say he's been missing for some time. How did they get on to him?' queried Cornfeld.

'His wife reported him missing. She's been in hospital these past three weeks. Car accident. When the PC carried out the routine house-search, he found a room full of vampire-type stuff. Even some kind of ghastly altar. There's no doubt at all in their minds. He's the chap.'

Cornfeld let out a deep sigh.

'That's it then. Mr. Vine, would you be good enough to come with me?'

Vine got to his feet at once.

'Of course. Going to see the wife, are we?'

Abe Cornfeld looked puzzled.

'The wife? Lord no. Waste of time. We can forget all that. The police are on to it. Nothing we can do that they can't do quicker, and better. We'd only get under their feet. Wouldn't want that, eh, superintendent?'

He gave one of his wicked little grins. He knew that Vine's thoughts would have been running exactly along those lines.

'Er, well no. Then what—'

'A splendid treat for us on a misty November night, Mr. Vine, a gentle stroll through an unlit graveyard.'

178

CHAPTER FOURTEEN

Abe Cornfeld drove slowly through the night streets. The fog was settling more heavily, now that the earlier breeze had dropped. Traffic was light, because the theatres and cinemas had not yet concluded their final performances of the day, and he made reasonable time until he reached the far end of the Strand, and worked his way around Aldwych into Fleet Street.

'Good job you're driving, Professor. I'm lost already,' commented Vine.

'We're in Fleet Street,' was the reply, 'heading into the City proper. The lighting won't be so good shortly. Nobody lives there, you see, or at least, very few people. Place is dead from six o'clock on.'

The superintendent wished he'd chosen his words more carefully.

Soon, they had left Ludgate Hill, and were crawling along Cannon Street. The fog here was noticeably worse.

'It's always quite bad here,' explained Cornfeld, craning his head over the wheel. 'We're getting closer to the river. Never mind, it could be worse. We could be on the River Police, eh?'

'Nice night for a spot of smuggling,' agreed his passenger.

'Got to turn right here somewhere. Can't see the other side of the road, never mind place names. Ah, I think that might be a turning.'

The car indicators glowed feebly, and Cornfeld began gently to turn the wheel.

'Blast.'

They were about to enter a gateway. Cornfeld backed around.

'I'm going to drive on this side of the road,' he decided. 'There's nothing about. If we get told off, that's too bad.'

The car inched forward again, until they came to a turning. The professor turned into it, and Vine was just able to make out a familiar sign.

'This is a no-entry,' he announced.

'Won't matter, at this hour. Place we want should be somewhere on the left. We'll get over there.'

A hundred yards further along, the kerb ended.

'Would you mind, Mr. Vine? See if you can spot the name-plate. Torch here.'

Vine clambered out, and peered up at the side of the building. There was a name-plate. He brought the torch into play. Vaguely, through the shifting mist, he could make out the words.

Wallock Street.

He went back to the car.

'This is it,' he grunted.

180

'Splendid. Here we go, then.'

They turned into the street, and moved steadily along.

'Wonder if we're near the end? See if you can spot a number, would you?'

Vine climbed out once more, searching for a doorway. Soon he was back.

'Number thirty-two. Tell you what, Professor, you're only going at walking pace anyway. I'll walk along beside you until the last building. What was the number again?'

'Sixty-eight.'

'Right.'

They resumed their snail's pace advance. Finally, Vine leaned in at the passenger window.

'We've arrived.'

Cornfeld grunted acknowledgement, switched off the engine, then the lights.

'We'll stay close,' he decided. 'This is no time for us to be separated.'

Ten yards along, Vine looked back towards the car. It had disappeared from view. There were no street lights now, and the world seemed to consist of a damp blanket of fog. The silence was eerie, broken only occasionally by the low moaning of a foghorn on the river.

Abe Cornfeld's face was grim and tense as he walked slowly, almost reluctantly forward. The ground to their left was broken now, and separated from the street only by a low wooden fence, more marker than barrier. He was looking for an entrance of some kind, and soon found it. A low wooden gate, standing crazily from broken, rusted hinges.

They had ceased conversation, each preoccupied with his own thoughts. Vine touched his companion on the arm, indicating the gate. They stepped through, onto damp lank grass which formed rough lines between the irregular, weather-stained gravestones. Vine removed the torch from his pocket, but Cornfeld restrained him, shaking his head. They moved forward several yards into the obscure night.

Vine jumped as his companion's voice spoke into the blackness, low but clear.

'We are here.'

They stood quite still, scarcely daring to breathe. For there was evil here. Both men could feel it, silent but menacing, surrounding them, plucking at their sleeves with icy fog-tendrils. A long minute passed, a minute which seemed an hour. Vine swivelled his head round every few seconds, his eyes trying to pierce through the pall.

They sensed the arrival rather than saw it. To their left, the fog seemed suddenly to swirl, and there was a figure. A black-clad, withered skeleton in the outline of a man. Vine caught his breath.

Nosferatu.

The three stood looking at each other.

Cornfeld did not need to be told of the newcomer's identity. It had to be the sinister creature who had made such a profound impression on the superintendent and his assistant at the outset. Any lingering doubts were dispelled by the voice, the quiet dry hissing which now reached them.

'Ye are not he who comes.'

Even yards away, and in that gloom, the eyes seemed to glow with unnatural intensity.

The professor's words sounded oddly out of place. Too normal for the situation.

'No, we are not. You think he will come, then?'

Skinny, crab-like fingers pointed at him.

'He will come. The blaspehemer will come. He must seek the peace only the Master can give. He knows this.'

Cornfeld's voice was firm.

'How can you be sure? He might be just a common criminal, a man whose mind is crazed. A man who does not realise what dark powers he meddles with.'

'That has been true. He was all those things. I warned you, did I not, policeman? I warned you to catch him, punish him. You did not. And now, it is too late.'

Vine cleared his throat.

'How d'you mean, too late?'

'He will be caught,' affirmed Cornfeld, 'and quickly.'

Nosferatu drew himself up, appearing to

gain height even as they watched.

'No. He will come. His punishment is here, not with you, creatures of Earth. By his meddling, he has lifted one corner of the veil. It is enough. Go from this place. Leave the blasphemer. You have no punishment for him. Save death. And that is none.'

Cornfeld took a pace towards the speaker.

'Now, you hear me, Nosferatu, if that be your name. You say this man has lifted a corner of the veil. I believe you, oddly enough. I too have lifted a corner of another veil. The one surrounding your efforts for the coming of your evil master. I am your enemy. Know me.'

'I see you, enemy.'

'Then know this. I have the power to remove this soil, this earth of Wallachia. To remove it one ounce at a time, and scatter it in the furthest depths of the ocean. This I will do, if you do not desist.'

There was silence.

'Is this true, policeman? Can my enemy do this?'

Vine was surprised at the strength in his own voice. 'Yes, that can be done.'

'And it will be,' supplemented Cornfeld.

'What is your price?'

The professor felt that there was a chance of success.

'Your Master sleeps. There is other soil. In other lands. Go there. Leave my land in peace. And this soil shall remain.'

184

When Nosferatu spoke again, he uttered one word, which seemed to slither and creep its way into the very fibre of the listeners.

'Hereafter?'

There was a pause. Then Cornfeld shook his head.

'I cannot promise that. I am mortal. I will die. You must know this. But I shall leave my words. I shall do what I can.'

Vine was striving to remove his eyes, away from the cold ferocity of the spectre's icy stare. In vain.

'What of the blasphemer?'

Cornfeld hesitated. For all he knew, Duncan might already be in custody.

'You do not answer.'

'I do not answer quickly, because I do not promise quickly. There are other men who seek him. If they find him, my promise is worthless.'

'But if they do not?'

'Then have him. Do what you must.'

'I, Nosferatu, make this bargain. You have heard me, policeman.'

'I have heard you,' repeated Vine.

The bony arms were raised sideways, making the figure seem like some huge evil bird, about to pounce on its prey.

'Then go, enemy.'

The arms crossed, shutting off the glow from those terrible eyes. Vine blinked. In that fraction of a second. Nosferatu was gone from

185

view.

'Where did he go, professor? I mean, so fast?'

'I tremble to think,' muttered Cornfeld. It was literally true, he was trembling from head to foot. 'I suggest we grope our way out of here.'

Neither of them commented on the noticeable increase in their pace.

CHAPTER FIFTEEN

Sue Duncan felt utterly drained. So soon out of hospital, she ought to have spent the first couple of days quietly. Accustoming herself to the change of pace, the environment. Instead of which, she had been subjected to a seemingly endless barrage of questions. One policeman after another had been pounding at her, until she thought her mind would burst. Then suddenly, it was all over. They'd all gone. Photographers, fingerprint men, all kinds of people. She hadn't even known what half of them were supposed to be doing. At the end, they'd wanted to leave her under guard.

'A guard? What for?'

'He could come back, madam. You might be in danger.'

'From Donald? Never.'

The chief inspector, or whatever he was,

frowned.

'Mrs. Duncan, I don't think you quite understand the position. If your husband was responsible for—for these things we think he might be, he isn't the man you think you know, at all. He's very dangerous.'

'No. Not to me.'

She'd been quite adamant about it. In the end, and mainly to get rid of the man, she'd agreed to let a woman officer spend the night in the house.

'The officer will come at ten o'clock, if that's convenient.'

'Very well,' she agreed listlessly.

'Meantime, we'll have an officer watching from outside, just on the off-chance that your husband might come home.'

'If you must.'

They'd gone away then. She thought about making herself another cup of tea, decided against it. She must have had six cups at least in the past few hours. There was some gin in the dining-room. Sue poured herself out a small quantity, and poured plenty of tonic water into the glass. Her mind was seething with developments. To think of Donald—Pah. She'd probably have it all again when the policewoman arrived. What was the time now? Nine o'clock. One hour. Do something completely different, that was the answer.

She picked up the circular leaflet from the cosmetics people, and slipped it out of the brown envelope, which she left on the table. Then she sat down, and tried to read about the new exciting eye shadows. But supposing he did come? Supposing he did get violent? She'd have no protection. Serve her right for refusing the guard. It would be better if she had a gun. What would be the use? She'd have no idea how to fire the thing, anyway. Probably blow off her own toe, or something.

Knife, though. Didn't have to be an expert to use a knife. How ridiculous, to think about having a knife handy, in case Donald came home. Nonsense. Some of these new colours looked as if they might suit her rather well. Particularly that Grecian Evening, that looked nice. Of course, there was that terribly sharp paper knife she'd brought back once, from a holiday in Spain. In the drawer of the dresser.

Three quick steps took her to the dresser. She took out the hideously decorated little knife, and stared at it. It was certainly sharp enough. That's why they'd decided not to use it, even for letter-opening. She went back and sat down again, the knife by her hand.

The telephone rang, out in the hall. More policemen, no doubt.

'Hallo.'

'Mrs. Duncan?'

A man's voice, rather pleasant.

'Yes, who is this?'

'We haven't met. My fault, I'm afraid. My name is Dalrimple. Donald and I—'

'Yes, of course, Mr. Dalrimple. Donald has often mentioned you. He's not here, I'm afraid. In fact—' she hesitated—'to tell you the truth, he's missing.'

'Missing? Oh dear, I am sorry. I haven't seen him for quite some time, you see. I've been ringing the house regularly, but no one's answered.'

'No, no they wouldn't. I've been away— away. Until today.'

'I see.'

There was a pause. Obviously the poor man didn't know what to say.

'Mrs. Duncan, I'm sure it's a frightful imposition at a time like this, but the fact is, Donald has some of our paperwork. It's making life rather difficult. I wonder if I could pop round sometime and have a look for it. Wouldn't take a minute, and it is rather important.'

'Yes. Yes of course, I quite understand. Well—er—'

'I wonder if I could come now? I'm quite close by, as it happens.'

Sue hesitated. There was some paper belonging to Donald up in his room. Well, why not. The house had been full of strangers all day.

'That'll be all right, Mr Dalrimple. Place is in rather a mess, I'm afraid.'

'I shan't notice. I'm most obliged. In about ten minutes, then.'

She put down the phone. Odd, really. Donald had never talked much about his new boss, and she'd often wondered about him. Still, Donald never talked much about anything at all. She'd be seeing him for herself in ten minutes.

Ten minutes. Her face.

Outside the house, and on the opposite side of the road, a police officer sat in a patrol car, listening to the radio. He'd learned that reading was a bad idea on watch, because you could get absorbed, and miss something. With the radio your eyes were free. Hallo, something seemed to be happening.

A car had drawn up outside the house, and a man got out. The officer could see him quite clearly, in the light from a street-lamp. Well, whoever he might be, he certainly wasn't Donald Duncan. Three inches too tall for a start, and those lean features could not be mistaken for the slightly chubby appearance of the wanted man. Who might he be, then? One of the boyfriends, probably. Mrs. Duncan seemed to be quite a lively lass, by all accounts.

Sue answered the door to a tall man in his middle thirties. Good-looking with dark smooth hair.

'Mrs Duncan?'

It was the voice she'd heard on the telephone.

'Mr. Dalrimple. Please come in.'

He followed her inside, and the door closed. The policeman relaxed. All right for some.

Sue led the visitor into the sitting room. Her glass looked very prominent.

'Er, I was just having a drink. Could I get you something?'

'No thank you, really. I don't want to intrude. This is an awful shock, Donald being missing. Have you told the police?'

'Oh yes, they haven't been gone very long, as a matter of fact.'

On the point of telling him of their suspicions, she checked herself. After all, if it proved to be nonsense, as she felt it would, there was no point in jeopardising his job.

'Well, I do hope they find him soon. Poor chap could be suffering from amnesia, or something.'

'Yes, well I hope you're right. I mean, I hope it's nothing more serious.'

'I'm sure it won't be. Er, did you have a chance to think any more about those papers?'

'Oh sorry, yes. I've put everything I can find on that table. Please help yourself to whatever you might need.'

'Thank you.'

Dalrimple walked across the room, and began to look at the correspondence. Sue noted the huge ring on his left hand. A massive mounting of some kind was set in what looked like beaten silver. The kind of ring people used to use for sealing letters in wax, in days gone by. Odd sort of thing for a modern, youngish man to be wearing.

'Oh, this envelope's addressed to you, Mrs. Duncan.'

He was holding the envelope from the cosmetics people.

'Oh sorry, yes.'

She held out her hand for it.

'That's odd,' he said, puzzled. 'I always thought Donald said your name was Susan?'

'Yes. what about it?'

'But this is addressed to Mrs. L. Duncan.'

'Ah, I see. Well, it's correct, really. Susan is my second name. I much prefer it, and all my friends call me by it.'

'I see. May I ask what your official name is, then?'

'If you promise not to tell anyone. It's Lucy.'

'Lucy.'

Dalrimple went very still.

*   *   *

Weston was on the telephone, listening carefully, when Abe Cornfeld and the superintendent returned from their nightmare expedition. Their only conversation since leaving the graveyard had been concerned with finding their way out of the fog. As though by mutual consent, neither had made any reference to the encounter with Nosferatu.

Cornfeld made straight for the kettle, to

192

find it empty. Weston made signs to indicate that the call was important. After a few minutes of waiting, he put down the receiver, and let out a long sigh.

'They've found him. Found Duncan.'

'Good.'

'Not good, actually. The man is dead. Been dead some days. The Glasgow police identified him at once from the wanted photographs that were put on the wire. They had him as an unidentified murder victim, till then. Stabbing job.'

'Some days?' Vine butted in. 'But then he couldn't have—'

'—committed the last murder. No.' Weston shook his head. 'And top level, that is Sir Eliot himself, has decided that since everything else fits, the whole of the Duncan pattern, then they have to trace his boss, and quickly. They travelled everywhere together.'

'What's his name, this new man?'

'I wrote it down. Here. Dalrimple. A.V. Dalrimple.' As he read it out, Weston's face went pale. 'My God.'

Cornfeld nodded.

'Yes, you're right, Weston.'

Vine was losing the thread.

'Right about what? What's going on, please?'

Cornfeld waved him away, thinking furiously. Weston said gently, 'It's an anagram, Mr. Vine. Chap's been telling us from the start who he is. Waiting for us to spot it.'

'Anagram?' repeated Vine, mystified.

'A.V. Dalrimple. It's Vlad Impaler.'

*   *   *

Sue Duncan didn't like the change on her visitor's face. His eyes had clouded over, and he was breathing rapidly.

'Lucy, did you say?'

'Yes. Is something wrong?'

A half-choked gasp from his lips as he turned haltingly towards her.

'You are she, are you not? You are Lucy. At last, Lucy.'

He took a step forward, his face working strangely. Sue put a hand to her lips, and caught her breath.

'Mr. Dalrimple—'

'Vlad. Oh Lucy my love, I find you at last. All the searching.'

She was now definitely alarmed. It was as though he wasn't seeing her at all, but looking inside her. For—what?

'Keep back,' she commanded.

'Fear nothing. Now, or evermore. For you shall dwell with me, in the dark shades of the netherland. There will be no death, now or ever. Not for you. Not for Lucy. They must have a body, the earth creatures. We shall give them that one. For you shall be free of it. Free to roam into the far centuries with your one

194

true love, I, Vlad Tepes, command it.'

The knife, She must find that knife. Ah, there. She snatched it up. He watched the movement, smiling thinly, his breath coming in long, slow exertions. He pressed at his huge ring, and a needle point sprang from the surface. His eyes seemed to glow, piercing into her, sapping the will from her limbs.

'A scratch, my love. No more. Then you shall be rid of your form. Free to stand at my side. Now, and always. Come.'

She took a step forward, the knife useless at her side. A second patrol car drew up beside the officer on watch. A young policewoman climbed out, carrying a small case.

'Thanks for the lift. Good night.'

"The second car moved off. The duty man got out of his own vehicle.

'Hallo, Katie. You spending the night with our client, then?'

'Yes. Hope it's a waste of time. Don't fancy getting my neck bitten very much.'

'All in the course of duty, love. I'll come in with you, if you like. Get you settled down. Might even bite your neck myself.'

The girl grinned.

'You're all talk, Andy. But come over anyway, will you? Just to see me in.'

'Pleasure.'

They walked across the road, chatting casually. Suddenly, there was a blood-curdling scream from the house. They began to run.

*   *   *

Vlad held out his ring-hand, the needle pointing inwards. Something seemed to snap in Sue's head. She shook herself, and jumped back in alarm. The knife came upwards, and she screamed, a thin animal wail that ripped through the night air.

Vlad paused, and wagged his head sideways.

'False,' he breathed. 'You are false. Like the rest. Not Lucy. Not she who is my all. Not Lucy.'

He lunged at her. She sidestepped away from the deadly needle, and struck upwards with the knife. It plunged into his side, and stuck there. He grunted with sudden pain, and wheeled towards her, the light catching the hilt as the knife protruded obscenely from his body.

There was hammering at the street door, and shouting. Sue fled into the hall, scrabbling at the catch. Two anxious, uniformed figures tumbled inside.

'He's—he's—'

She pointed inwards, and collapsed on the floor. The police officer rushed into the lounge, to find it empty. French doors stood open. He ran through into the garden, clutching for his truncheon. From the front of the house came the roar of a car engine. He was in time to see the rear lights disappearing down the road. Hurrying back inside, he checked that Sue Duncan was all right. Then he ran down the path, to the radio waiting in his car.

*   *   *

An hour had passed since the report from the Duncan house. Alec Vine had taken the unusual step of activating his police radio. Abe Cornfeld and he sat drinking coffee and listening to the direct service on the special frequency from the operations room at New Scotland Yard.

Voices crackled from time to time, as the latest reports and scraps of information filtered through. All forces had been alerted with the description of the murderer's car, and it was fairly certain that at one point it had been seen, heading eastward along High Holborn. Several high-ranking officers were puzzled by Sir Eliot's decision that there should be no watch kept between St. Paul's and London Bridge. They had not been privy to a conversation thirty minutes earlier, between Sir Eliot and Abe Cornfeld.

'I wish to make it quite clear, Professor, that I do this under the strongest protest. Your instructions will be obeyed, and to the letter. I guarantee that personally. But I shall make the circumstances quite clear in my report tomorrow.'

197

'I fully understand your position, Sir Eliot. Thank you for your cooperation.'

Cornfeld would have liked to explain himself, but there was no time. In any case, who would have understood? Or even believed him? He found it hard to believe himself.

'That's odd,' said Weston suddenly. 'I've been mapping those spot reports in my head. There's been nothing east of St. Paul's Churchyard. Nothing. Not until you get to the far side of London Bridge.'

Hearing this, Vine looked enquiringly at Cornfeld. That was the area they had visited, a few short hours before.

'Yes,' replied the professor quietly. 'I know.'

*   *   *

A white-faced man stumbled and grabbed at a jutting headstone. Blood dripped onto a faded inscription. Pulling himself upright, he staggered forward a few more yards.

'I have come,' he called, weakly. 'I have come.'

Then he saw a black-shrouded figure standing close, and watching him. He gazed deep into fathomless eyes, and sighed with relief.

'Atone,' he muttered. 'I must atone.'

'You are the one.'

A dry, sibilant voice filtered into his fading consciousness.

'What—what must I do?'

'There.'

A bone-like finger stabbed at the fog. A red haze was settling over the eyes of the dying man. He followed the direction of the finger. From a fresh-turned mound of earth, a needle point of wood reached up into the night.

'Ye know what must be done.'

'Shall I—rest?'

'There are no promises for such as ye. Do what must be done.'

Vlad made a supreme effort, pulling himself upright, and walked slowly forward.

'I come, Master,' he cried.

Closing his eyes, he toppled heavily onto the pointed stake.

In the distance, a dog howled, then was still.

We hope you have enjoyed this Large Print book. Other Chivers Press or Thorndike Press Large Print books are available at your library or directly from the publishers.

For more information about current and forthcoming titles, please call or write, without obligation, to:

Chivers Large Print
published by BBC Audiobooks Ltd
St James House, The Square
Lower Bristol Road
Bath BA2 3BH
UK
email: bbcaudiobooks@bbc.co.uk
www.bbcaudiobooks.co.uk

OR

Thorndike Press
295 Kennedy Memorial Drive
Waterville
Maine 04901
USA
www.gale.com/thorndike
www.gale.com/wheeler

All our Large Print titles are designed for easy reading, and all our books are made to last.